Kalan the Mighty Warrior

TO SETH —
I hope YOU ENJOY
The ADVENTURE!

Kalan the Mighty Warrior

Book One

Braxus The Owl--Guardian of the Forest

Written by Kim Strauss

iUniverse, Inc.

New York Lincoln Shanghai

Kalan the Mighty Warrior
Book One

iUniverse books may be ordered through booksellers or by contacting:

iUniverse
2021 Pine Lake Road, Suite 100
Lincoln, NE 68512
www.iuniverse.com
1-800-Authors (1-800-288-4677)

This is a work of fiction. All of the characters, names, incidents, organizations and dialogue in this novel are either the products of the author's imagination or are used fictitiously.

ISBN-13: 978-0-595-37360-4 (pbk)
ISBN-13: 978-0-595-81757-3 (ebk)
ISBN-10: 0-595-37360-7 (pbk)
ISBN-10: 0-595-81757-2 (ebk)

Printed in the United States of America

Kalan the Mighty Warrior is dedicated to my beautiful son, Kalan.
Thank you for helping me dream again.

I love you more,
Dad

Thank you Richelle for your loving support.
I could not have written this book without you.

&

Thanks to Tulipan, Bruno, Saunders and Bennett
For your friendship and great ideas.

Is all that we see or seem
but a dream within a dream...
Edgar Allan Poe

Contents

Prologue

Many centuries ago, there was a terrible fire that engulfed all of the forest and meadowland and mountains around us for hundreds of miles. Amongst the forest dwellers, it is now referred to as THE GREAT CLEANSING BLAZE. There was no escape for most creatures. It killed all of my family, my children and their mother.

I was hunting in the meadow when it began. As I ran towards my village to help, I quickly realized that I had no chance at all to save my family or my people. All I could do was try to save myself.

I ran to the water's edge to flee the deadly flames, but the heat was still too much for me to bear. I walked down into the cooling water to try to escape the fate that had already befallen my people. As I scooped up the water into my hands and raised it to soothe my burning face and eyes, I saw hundreds of innocent creatures running out of the blazing forest towards the water, on fire.

It was an inferno. There was no hope for escape for any of us. We were all trapped, surrounded by flames and smoke and falling, burning trees. I walked deeper into the water thinking it might be my respite, but I quickly realized that even the water was beginning to burn. Indeed, this was no ordinary fire. A world of black, suffocating smoke billowed and rose thousands of feet into the air so quickly that even the birds were choked by its force and sent plummeting to the ground.

I stood there in my final moments, realizing that the last of my kind was about to become extinct. Everything was dying around me. I fell to my knees waist deep into the water, and prayed my last prayer to my glorious Mother Earth. I prayed for guidance and strength as I felt the temperature of the water around me slowly rise, and my hair and scalp begin to burn from the falling cinders. As I continued to pray, not only for myself, but also for the creatures that were falling all around me, and for my family and loved ones, I heard a still, small voice in my head.

"What would you do if you were to live?" the voice asked me. "What would you pay for your life at this moment?"

"Anything!" I screamed as the water in the shallows began to boil. "Anything if you let me live, oh Great One!"

It spoke to me again, "You who are kind and gentle in spirit; you who have loved and respected my forests and meadows, my lakes and streams and all the creatures of the world; you who have truly cherished each moment of life, each breath of sweet air; you who have welcomed each drop of heaven's tears as well as the golden rays of the great star; if you trust in me now, and believe you are worthy, I will lift you up from this scorching death into the heavens above where you may rest your weary soul, and I will perch you on a pillowy cloud of pure white, where you will live to hunt another day. There is but one thing I ask in return."

"Anything," I replied.

"You will hunt for evil. You will fight for the innocents of the forest. For as long as you are needed, you shall be The Guardian. Agree to this, and you shall see the miracle," the voice said.

"I agree," I cried out desperately as the salt from my tears burned my face more than the surrounding flames. "I believe...I believe," I said. "I will help the innocents and fight for them...for as long as you wish."

As the fire closed in around me and my flesh began to burn, I closed my eyes and raised my hands to the sky above. I felt the scorching hot wind begin to swirl around my head as it moved down around my body. It was so terribly hot, at first, I thought I would perish, but quickly it began to cool. It began to whirl faster and faster around me, until I felt it start to pick me up out of the burning lake and raise me up into the sky. I was afraid to open my eyes. Was I kidding myself? I wondered. Instead of being saved, was this not what it must feel like to die?

I felt like I was being pulled apart. There was no burning pain anymore. It had been replaced by an odd feeling of heaviness and again, being stretched. To my amazement, I suddenly realized what was happening...I was growing! I was magically being raised above the burning forest below in a cool swirling wind...and I was growing! It was a miracle.

I opened my eyes to see that I was right. I was now high above the trees and even above the massive columns of smothering smoke and ash. I was so amazed, and so elated by this euphoric flight from death, that I had totally overlooked the most incredible part of this miracle...I had wings! Gigantic glorious wings. And my eyes...my eyesight was so keen, that I could see a small bunny at the edge of the burning forest at least 100 miles away. Not only could I spot this frightened little being, but I also heard its cry for help. I hovered there, above the clouds, with such sorrow in my heart for this doomed little creature. As a tear fell from my eye, and the pain in my heart began to grow, the small voice again spoke to me.

"You agreed to be The Guardian...BELIEVE."

At that moment, as I held the desire to help the bunny in my mind, another amazing thing took place. In the blink of an eye, I was suddenly hovering directly over the rabbit. I didn't remember flying there, I was just...there—in an instant, with the power of a single thought. I quickly dropped down to grab the terrified bunny and help it to safety. But as I reached out for it, it wasn't my hand that grasped it. It was a bird's talon...my talon. Was I dreaming? I wondered. Or was I dead?

With ease and wonder, I flew my new friend to the fresh water stream just across the meadow, away from the burning trees. As I placed him on the shore of the stream, I looked into the water. There, for the first time, was I introduced to my new self. I was not shocked as one might expect, I was in awe. I was alive. I was an owl. Not just an ordinary owl, but a huge, powerful and beautiful, magical owl.

I stared at my new reflection for hours. Within that time, all manners of creatures of the forest gathered to witness the miracle.

But not all welcomed the miracle. There were the dark creatures of the forest, and beyond, who did not believe in good and who wanted nothing more than to destroy me and everything pure and innocent. And while I prayed to the loving, kind and nurturing mother earth to save me, these creatures prayed to the shadow forces, the dark lords of the woods and field. They were turned into things you would not want to see. They are the ones I fight, and will continue to fight until another comes to take my place, or I am no longer needed.

Chapter 1

Knight Errant

Kalan was a smart little boy, always aware of what was going on around him with an understanding of things far beyond his years. Since the night of his birth his family had a strong feeling that he would be a very special child, because there was a blue moon in the sky that glorious night, which is a fairly unusual event. You see, a blue moon is the second full moon in a month when normally there is only one. An even more extraordinary event is a double blue moon, but more about that later.

Kalan lived in a northern suburb of Los Angeles with his dad, Frank, who had raised his ten-year-old son, with the loving help of the boy's grandma and grandpa, since he was a tiny baby; since the boy was three days new in fact and still in the hospital. A very strange account indeed.

Frank had arrived early to the hospital that third morning after his son's birth with a huge smile on his face, a beautiful bouquet of flowers for his loving wife and a brightly colored little stuffed dragon for his precious newborn son. How proud he was to be a new dad. Now forty-three years into his life Frank knew he was starting his family quite a bit later than most, but to him, Kalan couldn't have come at a better time. He was not only ready for this new adventure he was absolutely thrilled.

Frank strolled through the corridors of the hospital as if walking on a cloud, but as he walked into the room to greet his perfect little family his delight quickly turned into confusion. There on the bed, surrounded by pillows, was his beautiful little boy sleeping soundly, but completely alone. The baby's mother was nowhere to be found. He waited there in the room for her to return, thinking she was probably just walking the halls for a little stretch and exercise, but as the minutes passed and silence remained, a gnawing pain in the pit of his stomach convinced Frank that something was terribly wrong. His anxiety grew to be more than he could bear. He ran to the door and called for a nurse. Surely he was overreacting and the nurse would know exactly where his wife could be found. Maybe his wife had a test scheduled, he thought, or an appointment with a doctor of which he was unaware. With a confused look on her face, the nurse made it immediately clear to Frank, that she had no idea where his wife, Karrington, had gone and assured him that there was no test or appointment scheduled for her.

They frantically searched the halls of the hospital but could not find her. Security was called and they, along with several other hospital employees, searched the entire building including the basement, outside grounds, even the roof, and again, nothing. The search continued for weeks. Even with the help of the police department and local media, not even a single clue was left behind. Needless to say Frank was devastated. What could possibly have happened to his beautiful wife, the mother of his newborn baby boy? All he knew was that she was gone, without a trace, never to be seen again. Her disappearance is still a mystery to this day. But that my dear friends is another story all together. One I'm afraid we will not be able to address in this first tale.

So then, back to the story at hand…

Kalan was nine years old now and quite the explorer and adventurer. He never had any trouble keeping his day filled with exciting things to do. He loved to lie on his back in the soft green grass and watch the clouds as they changed shapes from elephants to birds to any number of wonderful things. His grandma Dee-Dee had told him before she died that this particular activity was one of the most important things a child could learn to do, and to never forget that. She said, "anyone who thinks that it's just silly folly and a waste of time doesn't know how to dream."

Kalan had lots of friends too, but there was also homework, and piano lessons. These were duties which he grudgingly performed at his fathers insistence, but he knew quite well that his father meant business when he told him, "no piano, no Playstation!" And so he did the homework, and practiced.

Then there were various sports activities such as soccer, baseball and basketball that his dad enrolled him in at his request. He was quite the athlete, and even at this early age was already sporting an impressive little six-pack on his thin muscular frame.

Kalan had his share of chores also, but one of his favorite fantasy pastimes was to pretend to be a great warrior, fighting off evil knights and giant winged dragons that were ever present and eager to invade and destroy his castle keep. Single-handedly he would wage his noble wars against these scoundrels; these wretched fire-breathing monsters that would take the very life of a lesser warrior. But Kalan, whose name actually meant "mighty warrior" in old Gaelic, would keep the wicked evildoers at bay with little more than courage and cunning.

He was also skilled in many forms of the fighting arts, including hand-to-hand and armed combat, and the strategies and tactics of warfare. In fact, he was an accomplished martial artist, and studied the secret and ancient teachings of the ninja, receiving the extremely rare and distinguished "White Star" belt; a rank that far surpasses that of the highest Black belt. It is an honor so extraordinary that it has been bestowed upon only one other individual in the history of the world—the only other recipient being none other than Odin, the god of war.

Kalan was also an expert archer; able to unload three arrows with a single draw, and let them fly simultaneously with incredible accuracy. Why he could hit a dragon flying full speed in a dive from 200 yards away, bringing it crashing down upon Dragonfly's Meadow, where his castle lies floating above the mist of the moors. In fact, he was just about to address another phantom foe, only this time pulling four arrows from his quiver, when his dad walked into his room.

"Are you ready for tomorrow, buddy?" his dad asked.

"Are you kidding? I can't wait, Dad," Kalan replied. "This is gonna be the best camping trip ever!"

"Well then you better start getting your things together, son," his dad said. "I'd like to leave bright and early tomorrow morning."

Kalan loved going camping with his father. They had been on many trips before, but this trip was going to be very different indeed. This would be far from what Kalan was expecting, or had ever experienced before. No, there would be nothing ordinary about this camping trip at all. You see, Kalan's birthday was less than forty-eight hours away, and although that in itself was a very exciting thing, there was something even more special about this particular birthday.

There was a long-standing family tradition, passed down through many, many generations of the O'Shel family. Much further back than any family member could possibly recall. Through the years, every first-born son of the O'Shel family was taken into the wilderness by his father on the eve of the boy's tenth birthday for some type of ancient ceremony. Kalan knew that this night was very important, although he had no idea what would actually take place. None of his cousins that had gone through the ritual themselves would tell Kalan about it. They had promised to keep it a secret and not give any information to any other O'Shel boy, for it must only be passed down from father to son, and any time Kalan tried to get his father to tell him even a little bit about what took place at this secret event, his father would just say, "you'll know when the time is right, Kalan. Trust me and don't worry about it, it's gonna be great."

Kalan didn't like the feeling of being left out but it was obvious to him that if he were ever going to find out the whole story, he would have to turn ten, and that time was only hours away. Soon, years of wondering and anticipation would finally be over. Kalan knew that he was about to experience something big...something wonderful and exciting, and he wanted desperately to be a part of it. He knew that whatever took place must be really extraordinary, because over the past few years he had witnessed the difference in a couple of his cousins when they had each returned from their secret night, somehow changed, and for the better. He also knew from overhearing them whisper from behind closed doors, that whatever it was they did at this mysterious gathering took place at midnight, around a fire.

If the truth be known, it's probably a good thing that Kalan couldn't make out all the secrets his cousins whispered about behind those doors, because it is hard to know how any nine-year-old boy would react after hearing the words, blood-oath.

Little did Kalan know what incredible adventures the day ahead would bring…a day filled with wonder and magic…and danger.

Chapter 2

The Weirdest Daydream

"Kalan," Frank called from downstairs.

"Yeah, Dad?"

"Why don't you give James a call and make sure he's packed and ready to go for tomorrow morning."

"Okay, Dad."

Kalan knew that James was every bit as excited about going on this trip as he was, because that's all his friend had talked about for the last month!

James was a stocky little dark-haired boy of Mexican Irish descent who had quite a unique talent that made him the envy of all his friends at school. He could shoot a stream of water through the space in his two front teeth, send it flying through the air, and soak a target over ten feet away. His buddies all thought it was a pretty radical skill. Every once in a while one of them would challenge James, only to end up cleaning the spittle off the front of their shirt.

Anyway, James was Kalan's classmate, best friend, cohort and most importantly Kalan's only equal when it came to wielding a broadsword or throwing an iron. In fact James' expertise at knife throwing was legendary in Dragonfly's Meadow and even more acclaimed in Wolfshire, which was where James' fortress was located, just seven miles north of Kalan's castle over the Black River Bridge. It was not as magnificent or grand a castle as Kalan's, but certainly every bit as majestic and impressive in its own right. It was more of a fortified manor house than a castle; considerably smaller, but quaint, and just as rustic. Extensive lawns and gardens, shrubs and trees of all kinds and glorious flowerbeds surrounded the house. For protection, a fifteen-foot high curtain wall made up of a variety of local stone, which was squarely hewn, encircled the property. There was an enticing path that led from the rear entrance of the mansion past ancient sculptures on the great lawn, then snaked its way through the largest of the rose gardens. At the edge of the property just inside the wall, where the crushed granite path appeared to end, sat a huge throne-like chair, which was carved from some sort of dark exotic wood. Behind the massive seat, however, was something quite extraordinary indeed, a secret door in the wall. The men who had built the stately manor were obviously extremely skilled masons because they were able to build the door out of solid stone and with very little effort it could be easily opened by the slightest push on a specific spot on the stone. It somehow pivoted in the middle, which created an opening on either side of the great stone that one could pass through. When the door was closed, however, it blended seamlessly into the wall making it virtually impossible to see, unless of course you knew exactly where to look. To top it all off, the outside of the wall and door was covered with dense thicket. It would be easier to spot a freckle under the feathers of a hummingbird as it darted from flower to flower than to notice this secret passageway.

As soon as Kalan got James on the phone and found out that he had been packed and ready to go for two days, the conversation switched over to strategic planning.

"Did ya pack your sword?" Kalan asked.

"Got it," James replied.

"And how about your dagger and shield?"

"Yep! Can we bring our slingshots?" James asked.

"As long as my dad says it's okay, and we're really careful."

"Oh man, this is gonna be so cool!" James shouted.

"Yeah," Kalan agreed "and we're going stay up past midnight tomorrow night and do something really neat around the fire," he added.

"All right, midnight!" James exclaimed, then thought for a moment before asking, "what do you mean something around the fire?"

"I can't tell you, James, but trust me, it'll be really cool."

"Why can't you tell me Kalan?" James insisted.

"It's a secret," Kalan whispered, "and, well…because I don't really know," he added almost choking on the words. Kalan felt a little embarrassed having to admit this to his friend, but after he told James the whole story, or at least what he knew of it, which of course was very little, James was even more excited than before.

Kalan knew exactly where his dad was going to take them. It was their favorite place to camp, truly a magical place. There was a beautiful, mountainous forest filled with tall cedars, fir trees and sugar pines, just to name a few, which sloped gently down into an azure blue lake packed with rainbow and brown trout just begging to be caught. Kalan and his dad had camped and fished there many times before, and although it was a type of secret spot hidden and isolated from the other campsites, Kalan felt comfortable with the area and pretty much knew his way around. Of course, he had always been under the watchful eye of his father. The sugar pines dropped huge cones, the largest cones of all the pine trees in the Sierras and some as big as Kalan's head. He used to love collecting these gigantic specimens and bringing them home. His dad however didn't like cleaning the sticky sap off the floor mats and once off the back seat, so he put a stop to that during their last trip. During the last couple of trips Frank and his son left their campsite during the day to visit some other incredible places in the sierras. On one of their day trips they drove to The Giant Forest in Sequoia National Park and saw the largest living tree in the world named General Sherman. This cinnamon colored member of the redwood family is over two hundred feet tall. Kalan was amazed when he stood under this gargantuan tree and looked up. It seemed to go on forever. The height of the first large branch was one hundred thirty feet above the ground!

As Kalan was visualizing the campsite and surroundings, and eagerly describing them to his excited buddy over the phone, something very strange happened, something Kalan had never experienced before. It was a feeling so eerie, it sent a cold shiver running down his spine. In the quickness of a moment, the hairs on the back of his neck stood on end and he watched in silent awe as goose bumps appeared all over his body. Weird and spooky images flooded his mind's eye. Pictures flew by so quickly that he wasn't even sure what some of them were, let alone what they meant. Black clouds, a rainbow with a tail, a ringed blue moon, and a shooting star. A huge snarling wolf walking upright on its hind feet. How creepy it was to see this monster, quickly tiptoeing towards him. Then all of a sudden, out of the blackness, a gigantic owl appeared clutching a short sword in his huge talons.

What could these things mean? Kalan wondered in quiet astonishment.

He was so confused. But before he had the time to be frightened, his trance was broken by a voice from the other end of the phone. "Are you still there, Kalan?"

"What?" Kalan asked, dazed. "Oh yeah, yeah I'm still here. Boy oh boy, did I just have the weirdest daydream," Kalan said as he gazed at the bright orange sun setting behind the mountains outside his second story bedroom window.

The seconds that passed seemed like minutes before James finally replied with his soft voice trembling, "was there a big wolf and an owl in yours?"

Chapter 3

Knight's Honor

With breathless wonder and amazement, the boys continued their eerie conversation. They knew enough to know that something strange had just happened between them, but they weren't quite sure just what. Was it mere coincidence that caused this fusion of thought, the sharing of a daydream? Or was it something much darker, more sinister at work here?

"I know what's going on!" exclaimed James.

"What?

"It's the black knight," James answered in a low whisper.

"The black knight, huh?" Kalan thought about it for a few seconds. "You really think so, James?"

"Yeah, I do," James continued to whisper. "Maybe he's really mad because the last time we fought him on the Black River Bridge we beat him so bad, we almost destroyed him."

"When was that?"

"Come on, Kalan!" James said firmly, annoyed with his friends memory lapse, "the last time I stayed over at your house...I mean castle." Then whispering again he added, "maybe he's back."

The boys had fought this black knight many times before but for some reason he was becoming more and more difficult to beat.

"He's getting stronger, James. That's what's happening."

Something dawned on James. "Remember the dream you told me about a couple weeks ago, Kalan? You were really freaked out 'cause you said it was so real."

Kalan remembered, but it wasn't a dream, it was a nightmare. He called his friend the morning after it happened, still wet with sweat. He told him that the evil knight actually spoke to him. "Do you know who I am, little man?" the evil knight asked him in a low threatening voice. "The time has finally come for you to find out. I am the one you must fear. I have waited patiently through the ages to exact my revenge on you, the mighty warrior," he said mockingly, "and your miserable family. You and your wretched kin will soon reach the end of your so-called royal bloodline. And the final battle will not take place in your little-boy dreams, but in your real world...where I've watched you. So sleep little knight, sleep...for as you do, I grow stronger."

"The Black Knight...yeah, well all the more reason to bring our swords then. Stupid-head dream anyway," Kalan bravely added.

Even with everything that had happened, the boys couldn't wait for the morning to come and the trip to begin. It was the kind of anticipated excitement that comes with watching a horror movie or riding a scary roller coaster. They were absolutely sure that this trip was going to be a very exciting trip indeed.

Just as James was about to say goodnight, Kalan interrupted with an idea. "Let's make a pact," he insisted. "Let's promise not to tell anyone what happened tonight, with the daydream, I mean. No one would believe us anyway."

"Yeah, you're probably right," replied James after a few seconds, then added, "okay, let's do it."

"Okay," answered Kalan, "I promise I'll never tell a soul about our daydream. Now you say it."

"I'll never tell anyone about our daydream, I promise."

"Knight's honor?" asked Kalan.

"Knight's honor," James promised.

And with that, the two buddies reluctantly ended their conversation and Kalan returned to his packing.

"Stupid dream anyway," Kalan muttered with a dismissive chuckle trying to convince himself it was nothing. "Stupid dream."

Chapter 4

Little Boy's Lullaby

Just as Kalan was finishing his packing, his dad walked into his room. "When you're done here, why don't you get your pajamas on, and brush your teeth and I'll tuck you in bed. We have a busy day tomorrow and I want to get an early start."

"Okay," said Kalan as he closed and fastened his suitcase. As his dad left his room, Kalan got up and did what his dad asked him to do, all the while, still thinking of the nightmare, the daydream, the images, the conversation with James and the promise. His head was spinning with weird, crazy, spooky, yet wonderful and exciting thoughts.

I wonder if James is thinking the same things I'm thinking? he thought to himself. *I wonder if he'll be able to sleep tonight...I wonder if I'll be able to sleep tonight?*

As Kalan brushed his teeth, he remembered how his father used to sing him to sleep with a lullaby, a song his Uncle Kurt wrote for his own son years earlier. *I bet that would help me to sleep,* he thought.

Just then his dad walked into the bathroom. "You ready for bed, buddy?"

"Just about, Dad," he answered. "Hey, Dad?"

"Yeah, Kalan?"

"Will you sing Little Boy's Lullaby for me tonight?"

"Little Boy's Lullaby?" his dad asked with surprise. "Wow, you haven't asked me to sing that to you in a while. I thought maybe you were too big or you didn't think it was cool anymore."

"Nope."

"Well then sure, Kalan, I'd love to."

"Great!" Kalan answered, as he put his toothbrush down, ran into his bedroom and threw himself onto his bed. His dad followed, smiling.

"Okay, buddy, get under the covers and I'll sing you to sleep," his dad said pulling the down comforter up to his son's chin. "I used to love singing this song to you when you were a little baby. I think it used to comfort me just as much as it did you."

"Really?" Kalan asked.

"Yeah, it sure did," his father said warmly as he leaned over and turned out the light. "I love you so much."

"I love you too, Dad," Kalan said reaching his face up for a kiss.

"I love you more," his dad whispered. And just as Kalan set his head down onto his flannel covered pillow and settled into his cozy bed for what was going to be a peaceful and restful night's sleep, his father began to sing.

"Close your eyes my little one,
Don't fear the night, your day is done.
You've conquered lands you've never seen
A king you've been without a queen."

"The curtains gently wave goodnight,
A summer breeze, the soft moonlight,
The world will sleep for one more day,
Your Kingdom keep while you're away."

"A father's prayer will comfort you.
No harm would dare come unto you.
God's angels stand guard by your bed,
While rainbow visions fill your head."

"With stars as stepping stones in the sky,
And pixie dust to help you fly,
Say hi to friends that I once knew
As earthly chains can not hold you."

"Some day you'll know just what it means
To watch you as you chase your dreams,
To love you and to see you grow,
You'll only just begin to know,
When soldier's toys are long on the shelf,
And the circle has completed itself,
And tonight is just a memory...
Still my little one you will always be."

"Goodnight my little one," Kalan's dad said in a loving whisper as he leaned over and gently kissed the forehead of his too quickly growing son. Realizing the preciousness of the moment, Kalan's dad remained motionless, listening—as the rhythm of his child's breathing began to slow and deepen, easing him ever closer to his castle in the clouds.

A few minutes passed as he reflected on the many beautiful times that he has been lucky enough to share with Kalan since his birth. After taking a final lingering moment to commit this image to memory, he got up and started for the door.

"Goodnight, Dad, I love you just as much," Kalan whispered softly from beneath his feather filled quilt, already halfway to dreamland.

Whereupon his father just smiled with a sigh of contentment, and without turning left the room, entrusting his only child into the loving arms of God's guardian angels.

Chapter 5

The Phantom Vision

Before morning's glow had a chance to intrude on Kalan's restful, unstirred slumber, his father was already dressed and waking his son, whose eyelids were still heavy with sleep.

As Kalan began to stir, his hand lightly brushed across his face as if wiping away any lingering dreams that might have come back with him from his journey into the land of Nod.

"Rise and shine," his dad said in a soft voice, lightly tickling his son's forehead and temples. "Good morning, buddy…did you have a good sleep?"

"Yes," Kalan replied in a faint voice as he slowly opened his eyes.

As usual, Kalan didn't whine about getting up in the morning no matter how early it was, which of course is just not normal for a child. Even after nine years Frank was still amazed how easy it was for him to get his son out of bed each day. Probably because he was the complete opposite when he was a kid, always complaining about rising early, or rising at all for that matter, and all the while driving Kalan's grandma crazy. Each and every morning Dee-Dee would try her best to wake Frank by starting with a sweet and soft "rise and shine" but after many attempts, would end up pulling the covers off of him while yelling, "LET'S GO...HIT THE DECK!" Even then Frank would roll out of bed with a grunt of annoyance and then wander through the house like a zombie. He remembered how, every school morning, his mom would have to constantly stay on top of him and his brother leading them around the house until finally she could push them both out the door to catch the bus with only seconds to spare. To this day it still takes a good forty-five minutes or so, and two strong cups of coffee, to really bring himself back to life each morning.

What time is it, Dad?" Kalan yawned.

"It's four a.m.," his dad answered as he turned on the light and walked towards his son's closet. "I told James' mom that we'd be by to pick him up around five, so we need to get you dressed and have a little breakfast," he added, handing his son his favorite blue jeans and soccer jersey. "Get dressed and I'll meet you downstairs in a few minutes," he said as he walked down the hall from Kalan's room towards the kitchen.

As Kalan rolled out of bed, he stretched his lean little arms as far as they could go up over his head and yawned again. He gazed past the jungle-theme curtains, which were gently waving in the soft sweet breath of morning, out his bedroom window into the darkness of the early morn. How calm and peaceful it all seemed. The distant mountains were beginning to faintly reveal themselves. The illumination from the streetlight down the block cast shadowy figures on the cold, dew-laden ground below and the gentle morning breeze made them seem as though they were alive.

Just then, something drew Kalan's attention to the hillside just beyond the streetlight. *Is that a coyote?* he wondered, a small chill again running down his spine. "Oh, it's probably just Max," he muttered to himself.

Max was the neighbor's big and friendly but highly over strung 90-pound Labrador Retriever from up the street. He would get out every once in a while and enjoyed wreaking havoc on the neighborhood garbage cans.

Kalan leaned forward, placing his hands on the windowsill, squinting his eyes hoping it would help him focus better on what he now thought was looking back at him! *This couldn't possibly be a coyote*, he thought, *they're much smaller. It can't be Max either, it's just way too big.*

Maybe he was right, but at that moment, he gazed even harder and thought he saw this huge dog, or whatever it was, begin to stand straight up on its hind legs and tiptoe eerily towards him while still looking at him, only now, with glowing red eyes.

Those eyes...dreadful, red eyes that pierced the darkness of this early morning...eyes that seemed to see him even from such a distance. The most frightening eyes Kalan had ever seen!

Pushing himself away from the window with a start, Kalan stood up and turned toward the bedroom door.

"Dad, Dad, come here quick!"

Hearing his son's scream, Frank flew up the stairs and ran into Kalan's room.

"What is it, Kalan, are you alright?"

"Outside, it's outside, Dad!"

"What? What's outside?" his dad demanded as he rushed over to the window his eyes quickly scanning the grounds below.

"Right there, Dad, across the street!" Kalan yelled as he pointed toward the window, but turned away from it.

"Where, what am I looking for, Kalan?" he asked, confused with his son's unusual behavior.

"It's coming right for the house!" Kalan shouted again.

"Settle down, buddy, there's nothing out there," Frank said trying to calm his son. "Come over here and take a look for yourself. Probably just the shadows from the trees playing tricks on you underneath the street light."

Skeptical, Kalan leaned back towards the window to get one last look, but his dad was right, nothing was there. It was gone. No dog, no coyote, nothing unusual. Kalan rubbed his eyes in disbelief.

"It's no big deal, son, you just weren't fully awake yet. You still had one foot in dreamland, that's all," his dad added with a smile.

"Wow," Kalan murmured along with a sigh of relief. "I can't believe it. I guess it must've been the sleep in my eyes, or just a shadow or something," he agreed while trying to convince himself that it was nothing. "Sorry, Dad."

"It's okay, buddy, don't worry about it," Frank replied as he grabbed his son and kissed the top of his head. "The same thing used to happen to me all the time. It used to drive Dee-Dee nuts.

Now hurry up and get dressed and meet me downstairs. I think I smell burned waffles."

"Okay, Dad, I'll be down in a minute," Kalan answered.

But before he could join his father for breakfast Kalan had to brave one last look from his second-story window, just to make sure nothing out of the ordinary was out there. But could this creature really have been just a figment of a boy's vivid imagination or some lingering dream vapor? It seemed so very real. Uncertain and a bit fearful he looked again…and again…nothing.

"Whew! Well, I guess it was just my sleepy peepers," he said with a chuckle as he ran downstairs for breakfast.

How fortunate for the child that as he turned to make his way downstairs, he missed seeing those piercing, glowing red eyes staring up at his window, as they slowly retreated back into the darkness of the early morn.

Chapter 6

The Trip

This is gonna be so incredible, he thought as he ran downstairs pulling up his jeans. *I'll be able to show James all the really neat hiding places around the campground and the best spots to build a fort. We can fight evil knights and dragons, and go fishing and hiking.*

After they ate, Kalan and his father loaded the rest of their supplies into the trunk of the car, and headed over to James' house. To their surprise and Kalan's delight, James was already waiting outside in the chill of the early morning, under the glow of the front porch light. Next to him was his suitcase, a sleeping bag, and of course his sword and shield.

Kalan flew out of the car and up to the porch where James and his mom were standing. "I'll take this for you," he said grabbing his buddy's sleeping bag.

"He woke me up at 3:30 this morning, telling me he needed to hurry up and get ready," his mom said, still in her robe. "I guess you could say he's excited," she added with a smile.

With that, James picked up his sword and shield and ran towards the car, leaving the suitcase for Kalan's dad to fetch.

"James...aren't you forgetting something, young man?" his mom asked sternly, stopping him dead in his tracks.

James, a little embarrassed, made a slow turn and answered shyly with a smile, "Oh yeah, sorry, Mom." He ran back up the stairs to the porch and hugged his mom, kissing her on the cheek.

"You'd better be a good boy, and listen to Kalan's dad," she told him. "Do you understand?" she asked, looking directly into his full, dark brown eyes.

"Yes Ma'am," he replied respectfully.

She took her son's face in her hands and tenderly kissed his forehead. "I love you...now go have a good time," she said as she turned him around and sent him off towards the car with a gentle push and a pat on the butt.

Once Kalan's dad checked to see if the boys were comfortable and securely belted in, he carefully backed out of the driveway, and they were off.

"Finally," Kalan anxiously sighed, "we're going camping!"

"Oh yeah!" exclaimed James. "This is gonna be so cool."

"How long till we get there, Dad?" Kalan asked.

"Okay," Kalan's dad said with a chuckle, "I was wondering how long it would take before we got to that. Now listen up...first rule," he lightheartedly demanded, "I don't wanna hear any, 'Are we there yet?' coming from either one of you swashbuckling tenderfoots, understood?"

The boys just laughed. "Okay, Dad, sorry," Kalan replied.

"It's about a five-or six-hour drive, so just make yourselves comfortable, and enjoy the company and the beautiful scenery, and we'll get there when we get there," Frank added.

The boys looked at each other and smiled, and with a sigh of delighted surrender, proceeded to settle in. The next few hours passed quickly and easily, with the boys, and occasionally Kalan's dad, playing car-games.

Just within the last half-hour or so, the drive had brought them into the lush and beautiful foothills of the High Sierra Mountains; very different from what they were used to in the high desert climate. The air up here was cooler and seemed cleaner, and actually smelled a little sweet. By eight o'clock that morning they had driven almost two hundred fifty miles, were pretty "gamed out" and ready for a fill-up and a much needed restroom break. So they exited the highway and pulled into the next gas station.

"We're making pretty good time," Frank said as he merged back onto the highway. "I think we can get to the lake in another hour and a half or so. You guys can help me out by keeping your eyes peeled for a sign that says Rainbow Falls. We'll take that exit northeast about forty five minutes till we get to a place called The Devil's Sugarbowl. From there on in, it's a beautiful winding mountain road that'll lead us straight to our campsite on the lake. You guys excited?" he asked.

"Devil's what?" James asked timidly.

"It's just the name of a place," Kalan said, chuckling as he comforted his friend with a pat on the shoulder. "It's really pretty through there. That's where I saw my very first bald eagle," he added.

That perked James right up. "I've never seen a bald eagle," he said.

"Well I'm almost sure you'll see one on this trip," Kalan's dad told him. "There are quite a few of them where we're going, along with bears, deer, cougars, wolves, owls, foxes and lots more.

The area is just teaming with wildlife. As a matter of fact," he added, "you might be able to see one close up. I was thinking about stopping at the rest area that has a little museum in it. It's about forty-five minutes away, by Rainbow Falls. We stopped in there on our last trip, Kalan, do you remember?"

"Oh yeah, I remember," Kalan quickly answered. "That'd be great, Dad." Kalan turned to his friend. "It's really neat there, James. They have a bunch of hurt animals in the back that they're trying to help. You can see them close up," Kalan told James.

"That's right, they're trying to nurse them back to health, so the animals can be released back into the wild where they belong. It's called a rehabilitation center," his dad informed them.

James was excited at the prospect of seeing his first bald eagle, even if it was in a cage at a rest stop. The boys were getting very anxious, which made the time seem to creep by.

"Not much further now, guys," Frank said, sensing the boy's excitement. The turn-off for Rainbow Falls is just ahead," he added as he veered off the four-lane highway and merged onto a much smaller two-lane road, thick with pines.

As they pulled up to the rest area, an excited Kalan quickly released his seatbelt. "Last one in is a rotten egg!" he shouted as he flung open the door, and bolted for the building.

Kalan's dad looked at James in the rearview mirror. The little boy's eyes were wide and his eyebrows raised. "Wow," he said in a calm sweet voice, "didn't give us much of a chance, huh?"

"No, I guess not," Kalan's dad laughed. "Come on, James, let's go inside and see what kind of animals they have around here, shall we?"

They got out of the car and made their way inside…completely unaware of what would be waiting for them when they returned.

Chapter 7

Paw Print and Feather

Having the entire place to themselves, except a single attendant, they spent the next thirty minutes or so learning all about the native wildlife. They even had a few small aviaries outside in the back of the building that housed a hawk, an owl and even a bald eagle. They had all been injured in one way or another, and were not yet healthy enough to be released.

"Well, I didn't think this would be the way you'd see your first bald eagle, James...in a cage, but you couldn't get much closer to one than this," said Kalan's dad.

"I didn't know they were so big, Dad. They look so much smaller when they're in the air."

Ordinarily, the boys could have spent hours there just watching the birds and browsing the facilities, but not today. They were much too excited about getting to the lake, fishing and, of course, Kalan's birthday. They just wanted to get to the campsite as soon as possible. Actually, Kalan wasn't as excited about his approaching birthday as he was to finally find out what the mysterious family ritual was all about. For some reason he had the strange idea that the sooner they got to camp, the sooner midnight would roll around.

As they walked back to their car, which sat alone in the dirt lot amongst the towering pines, Kalan's dad saw something on the roof of the car, just above the rear window where Kalan had been sitting, that wasn't there before. It was a huge muddy paw print. It looked as though maybe a large bear had leaned up against the car to get a look inside. It really appeared to be more like a dog print than a bear, but by the size of it, Frank knew that couldn't be possible. It was much too big for that. He quickly surveyed the area, while telling the boys to get inside the car.

"Dad, look!" exclaimed Kalan, as he reached for the door handle. "There are footprints on the ground too." The three stared in amazement at the huge impressions made in the ground just outside the car.

"Yes sir, those are wild animal tracks all right," his dad agreed, crouching down for a better look. "Mighty big ones at that. Wow...looks like there's a little blood here too. Hmmm...I wonder what happened," he thought out loud. "You know what?" he continued, coming quickly to a conclusion, "Someone...or something...must've chased off whatever it was. But by the looks of this bloody print, it didn't leave without a fight. This is so weird," he added as he stood and cautiously followed the trail of prints that led from the car to the forest.

"It looks like whatever it was walked on its back legs for about ten or fifteen feet before it finally went down on all fours and ran back towards the woods over here." He pointed as he walked to a spot about ten feet from the edge of the forest. There the enormous paw prints seemed to disappear. "Wow, that's really strange," he said as he lowered his arm and stared into the mysterious darkness. "They just disappear into thin air...almost like, whatever it was, flew away or something."

James felt a cold chill, as goose bumps appeared on his arms. "Kalan," he whispered so only his friend could hear, "remember our daydream?" he asked, as their faces grew pale.

"It has to be a bear," Kalan's dad guessed as he continued the investigation, "but it sure doesn't look like any bear prints I've ever seen. Too narrow. Looks more like wolf tracks. I'm almost sure that they're wolf prints...but they're huge," he said while removing his baseball cap to scratch his head in bewilderment.

"Well boys, this is a wilderness area we're in," he added, brushing the dirt off his hands as he walked back to the car, "so there's always the possibility of running into some wild animals. That's just part of the beauty and the wonder of getting away from the big city and becoming closer to nature."

Noticing that Kalan and James were a bit freaked out by his words and by what had just taken place, he smiled and added, "Trust me guys, animals are much more afraid of you, than you are of them. You just always need to be aware of your surroundings, and on this trip make sure you two stick together."

As Kalan reached for the door handle again, he noticed something just barely peeking out from underneath the car, partially hidden by the tire. He reached down to grab it. It was so long, that he actually had to back up as he pulled it out from its resting place. As he did, his eyes grew bigger and bigger with wonder and surprise, and his mouth dropped open in awe as he finally realized what it was.

"Holy cow, look at this!" Kalan cried.

"Is this real, Dad?" he asked with astonishment. "It…it can't be real…can it?"

James looked on in total disbelief, his mouth wide open.

"Are you kidding me?!" his dad said with equal amazement. "Let me take a look at that thing, buddy."

Kalan carefully passed the item to his father who then examined it thoroughly. What Kalan's dad held in his hand was a feather, except this was like no ordinary feather any of them had ever seen. This feather…was over four feet long!

"Man oh man," his father whispered to himself, not quite sure what to believe. "I've never seen anything like it. It looks like an owl feather. How's that possible?" he added, stunned with his son's discovery. "I know there are Great Gray Owls up here in the sierras, and they're one of the largest owls in the world," he said staring at the enormous quill, "but this is remarkable. I…I just don't know what to say." He opened the trunk and gingerly placed the massive feather down diagonally, which is the only way it would fit.

As they got back into the car to drive the final minutes through the breathtakingly beautiful Devil's Sugarbowl to their campsite on the lake, not a word was spoken. As the clouds drifted by in a baby blue sky up above, the frazzled boys stared at each other in silence, both contemplating their shared daydream and all that had just happened at that brief but magical stop. At the same time they swallowed nervously, with an audible…"Gulp!"

Chapter 8

Ahhh, Camp...
Hey, What The Heck Was That?

They drove down the last twenty feet or so of paved road onto the winding gravel drive that led to the campsite. As the car weaved its way through the thick forest of pines, cedar and redwoods, past a small clearing filled with beautiful wildflowers that surrounded a one-room log cabin, the boys temporarily forgot about their mysterious stop, with their first glimpse of the lake. They quickly sat up and stretched their necks to get a better look, but before you could say "Micklemoor Meadowcroft Pretty Penny Lane," the lake was gone, swallowed up by the dense timberland. Only teasingly would she reappear in alluring flickers through the trees as the dirt and gravel crunched beneath the tires that carried them ever closer to their enchanted destination.

"Here we are, boys," said Kalan's dad as the car rolled to a stop. They gazed out over the pristine, island-studded lake. "Pretty spectacular isn't it," he said as he let out a long contented sigh, with the slightest of smiles adorning his face.

As they sat there in silence and awe, the moment was interrupted by the sound of a single distant howl.

"What was that, Dad?" asked a wide-eyed Kalan.

"Probably just a coyote letting his family and friends know they have company."

"You mean…us?" Kalan asked with a fearful gulp.

"Yes, Kalan, I mean…us," he answered, playfully mocking his son.

Kalan's head snapped towards James, whose eyes were bigger still. They just stared at each other. Then suddenly, another howl. "HAHOOOOOO."

"Sounds like it's getting closer, Dad!" Kalan said, getting spooked.

"Ahh don't worry about it, Kalan," his dad replied dismissively. "It's not gonna hurt you. It's probably just curious, that's all," he added, hardly convincing the boys.

"Well, what do you think, James?" Kalan's dad continued. "Is it everything Kalan said it was?"

"Huh? What? Aahh yes…sir, it…it sure is," he answered with a rabbity whisper, obviously scared.

"Man, what's with you guys?" Kalan's dad asked with a chuckle. "What happened to the two fearless, sword-wielding dragon slayers I had in the back seat of my car about an hour ago? What'd you do, eat 'em? Come on guys lighten up for crying out loud. I think you guys have been watching too many scary movies lately. Listen, we're gonna be camping and fishing on this gorgeous lake in the middle of the Sierras…snap out of it already! Hey, wait a minute I have an idea," he added with a smile, as he opened the door to get out. "After you two are done freaking out back there, maybe you could 'cough up' the two brave knights I drove up here with. I sure could use some help unloading the car and setting up camp."

The boys looked at Kalan's dad, then at each other. Tension eased and feeling rather silly, they burst into laughter.

"Come on, man," Kalan said with an impish smile. "Let's go have some fun!"

"Yeah let's go," James said, playfully pushing Kalan from the car. "I'm not afraid of some stupid 'big butt' coyote!" They all laughed.

As Kalan's dad opened the trunk to unload the camping gear and fishing equipment, he was eerily reacquainted with the enormous feather Kalan had found earlier. "Boy, oh boy, how could I forget about you?" he said under his breath, hypnotized by the sheer size of it.

He reached down into the trunk and picked the feather up, being very careful not to damage it. "I just can't believe how big this thing is," he said to the boys as he laid it down across the entire back seat of the car. "It's got to be some kind of a record. I can't even imagine how large the bird must be that lost this thing. I sure wouldn't want to make him angry."

He folded a blanket over the plumage to hide it from any nosey campers that might peer into the vehicle unannounced. Locking the door, he turned to the boys and said, "Well, that'll be safe there until we leave. It's not going anywhere. Okay, let's get started."

They each grabbed something and walked it over to the campsite. Within thirty minutes, the tent was standing, and sleeping bags were arranged. A propane stove, lantern and cooking utensils were placed on the picnic table, which they had already covered with a plastic red-checkered tablecloth, and chairs were set up around the fire pit.

"Looks like home to me. What do you think, boys?"

"Great!" said Kalan.

"Really neat," added James.

"How 'bout we finish off those sandwiches I made, and then we head down to the lake and catch us some fish?"

"Yeah, let's go fishin!" they wholeheartedly agreed.

~   ~   ~

Did you ever notice how easy it is sometimes to block out unpleasant thoughts from your mind when something new and exciting is about to happen? Or even ignore things that you know are important, like homework, chores or maybe…oh, I don't know— let's say a giant feather and spooky daydream…when there's something fun to do instead? Well that's pretty much what Kalan and James let happen.

But they'll remember. Oh yes indeed, they will remember…soon enough.

Chapter 9

A Fish for the Reigning King

After a quick lunch, they grabbed their fishing gear and headed down to the water. The lake and surrounding area were breathtaking. It was so peaceful, unlike the clamor of the city. All you could hear was the sound of nature; the wind whistling through the trees and rustling the leaves, frogs croaking, and birds singing above, while an occasional fish would jump in the crystal clear waters of the bay just beyond their campsite.

"First one to catch a fish is king," said Kalan.

"How about the second one?" asked James.

"He's a knight!" Kalan answered without hesitation, confident he'd be the king.

"How about the third?" Frank asked.

The three looked at each other for a moment.

"The queen!" yelled James just beating Kalan to the punch.

They all laughed.

Just then, Kalan felt a tug on his line. "I got one!" he shouted.

"I think I do too," his dad said just as excited.

"Bet mine's bigger, Dad."

"Ha! You think you can out fish the pro do 'ya? Well, we'll soon find out, buddy," his dad replied, reeling in his line only to find Kalan's line tangled up in his. "Well, we caught something alright, but not exactly what I had in mind. I think we should throw these two back, what'ya say, Kalan?" his dad asked with a chuckle.

"Do we have to?" Kalan replied, going along with the joke.

As Kalan watched his father attempt to untangle the knotted lines, he caught a glimpse of something moving out of the corner of his eye. He turned his focus skyward just in time to see a Bald Eagle navigate its landing into a tree just a short distance away from where they were fishing.

"Dad, James, look quick! There's a Bald Eagle."

At that moment, all heads quickly turned towards the treetops where Kalan was pointing.

"Is that cool or what?" Kalan asked, nudging James with his elbow.

"It sure is," his dad answered with a smile.

"Wow," was all James could muster upon seeing his very first Bald Eagle in the wild.

While the large bird of prey perched itself on the top of the tall pine, the three of them watched still as statues.

"There you go, James, I bet you'll remember this moment for the rest of your life," said Kalan's dad, breaking the silence, but holding his gaze. "Just that in itself was worth the trip up here, wouldn't you boys agree?"

But before either of them could answer, James let out a squeal. "I got one! I got a fish!"

"Reel him in, buddy," shouted Kalan. "Reel him in!"

"Bring it in nice and steady now, James," Frank said. "Don't give the line any slack, keep it taut."

All eyes were glued on the end of the line where it entered the water.

"What kind of fish do you think it is, Dad?" asked an excited Kalan, just as the fish's tail broke the surface of the water. "Whoa, did you see that?" he added.

"I don't know yet. It's hard to tell, but it sure is putting up a good fight, huh, James?"

"Yes sir!" James answered through a huge smile.

The sun glistened off the animal's skin as he reeled it closer to shore. The moment was thick with anticipation and the boys' hearts pounded as they experienced the thrill of the catch.

"There it is!" Kalan cried.

"What kind is it?" asked James.

"That, my young fishermen, is a rainbow trout. See that beautiful rainbow coloring on its side? It's a good-sized one too. Well done, James," Kalan's dad said, praising the boy as he patted him on the back. "Well done. How did it feel?" Frank asked, pulling the fish from the water.

"It was unbelievable," James answered, then quickly added, "did you see how much it fought? Did you see its tail come out of the water when I was bringing it in? It was really strong! I think it almost got away, but I just kept reeling it in like you said to do and kept the line tight like you said, and look! I caught a fish…hey, I caught the first fish…I'm the KING!" He shouted with a big grin.

"Man, was that cool," Kalan said, a bit envious but still being supportive. "I want to catch one too, Dad!"

"Don't worry, there's a lot more where that came from, guys. But first, let's let this one go, okay? Catch and release, that's how we always fish up here, James," Kalan's dad explained as he gently placed the fish back into the lake and they watched it swim away.

A few moments later, Kalan's dad turned and reached for another worm to bait the hook. As the boys' attention remained transfixed on the spot in the shallows where the trout had just been set free, they noticed the water begin to gently ripple and swirl. Slowly and very eerily, the image of a wolf's head appeared on the surface.

Startled, the boys jumped back and looked at each other. Kalan turned toward his father to see if he also shared this strange vision, but saw that he was too busy wrestling with a slippery, yet tantalizing, night crawler to be aware of what was happening to the boys.

When Kalan turned back towards the water, he and James saw the wolf's head begin to slowly dissolve and transform itself into the shape of an owl. Its wings were outstretched as it silently soared through the sky. Kalan dropped his pole and brought his fisted hands up to his face to rub his eyes, as if he could wipe away the image. Puzzled by the vision, James picked up his friend's pole and handed it to him without a word. The next few moments were spent just staring at each other. Neither boy knew what to say.

"Boy, that's some cloud," Kalan's dad said, breaking the silence, unaware of the boys' fright.

The boys quickly turned their gaze skyward to see an ominous black cloud hovering over the lake.

"I've never seen a cloud quite like that before," Frank said. "It's pitch black. That is really unusual," he added.

The boys' heads turned slowly to face one another again, and then back to the water where they had just seen the wolf's head morph into an owl. Only now, in its place was the reflection of the cloud. The cloud was black, alright, so black that its reflection looked like a hole in the water. As the vision took hold of the boys, and they became lost in the darkness and depth of the hole, something else began to creepingly materialize.

"Boy, I'll tell ya what," Kalan's dad said, snapping the boys out of their stare. "I think this might actually be a good omen…Yep! That's what I think it is. It's a good omen. This is really turning out to be one heck of a camping trip, huh?"

"I'll say," Kalan said softly to James.

"Now let's catch some big ones boys!" Frank said as he handed James the pole with a freshly baited hook.

Within the next few hours the boys were pretty much able to forget about their secret, each catching more than their fair share of fish, which made all three very pleased. James, of course, won the title of "KING" by being the first one to catch a fish. Kalan was the proud runner up and happy to be called "KNIGHT," which then left the honorable but dubious title of "QUEEN" to go to none other than Kalan's dad. The boys had more than a few chuckles over that, especially when Kalan's dad did his impression of the queen's voice as he knighted his son using his fishing pole, and then bowed to James…the reigning king.

Chapter 10

Hero Talk

"Now that's what I call fishing!" Frank shouted with a smile. "Not like sitting around all day with your pole in the water without even getting a bite, wondering if there's any fish in the lake at all. Am I right, or what?" he asked as the boys smiled in agreement. "Okay, gather all your gear and meet me up at the tent. You guys can help me get dinner ready. Once we've eaten and cleaned everything up, we can get a fire going, make some s'mores—tell some stories and relax 'til midnight comes around. What d'ya say, guys?"

The boys looked at each other and smiled.

"Great!" Kalan replied thinking ahead of his birthday and the mysterious ritual to come.

The next several hours passed quickly, and before they knew it, night had gently pushed day aside. The s'mores were great, the stars were twinkling in the cool night air, and the fire was warm. Kalan loved the feel of the heat from the fire on his feet, occasionally pulling them away when it became too much.

"Why don't you back away from the fire just a bit, Kalan, before your shoes melt," Frank said with a smile, as James chuckled.

As the time drifted by, they talked about everything from school and sports to war, fear, and heroes. Every now and then Frank would have to get up to stoke or feed the fire. Now was one of those times, and as he reached for a log from the small bundle behind his chair, Kalan spoke.

"How does someone become a hero, Dad?"

"Good question, Kalan," Frank said as he tossed the cedar log onto the fire. He thought for a moment before continuing. "Well, son, in my opinion, a hero is someone who does the right thing no matter what the consequences may be. For instance, a person who rushes into a burning building to save someone, even though they know that by doing so, they may be hurt or killed. I think that's a pretty good example of a hero."

"Would you be afraid to do that, Dad?"

Frank smiled as he answered, "Well yeah, Kalan, I'm pretty sure I'd be afraid to do something like that."

"Me too," James said with his eyes still fixed on the fire.

"Yeah," Kalan agreed as he played with his lower lip. "I guess I'd be afraid too."

They sat quietly before the fire for several minutes, absolutely mesmerized by the dancing blue, white and gold flames. The crackling from the fire grew so loud; it drowned out the calming rhythmic sound of the crickets. But as the crackling subsided, and the bug-ballad began to return, Kalan asked, "Is it bad to be afraid of something, Dad?"

"Well I guess that would depend on what you were afraid of, Kalan," Frank answered. "Hey listen, guys," he sat up in his chair to make a point. "Everybody, at some time in their lives, is afraid of something. There's nothing wrong with being afraid, especially if there is a valid reason for that fear. True fear is a natural instinct— everybody is born with it. It makes you acutely aware of what's going on around you. It tells you that danger is at hand, and you'd better be careful."

"Heroes are never afraid though, right, Dad?"

"Wrong, Kalan. That's exactly what makes a hero, buddy. Let me try and help you two understand this, because it's very important." Frank took a few seconds to collect his thoughts, and after a deep focused breath, he continued. "Look, natural fear is supposed to be a good thing. It's a normal function of the body as a defense against danger, that dates back to the caveman."

By their confused looks, Frank could tell that the boys needed just a little more explanation.

"It's what tells you to get the heck off the tracks when there's a train coming at ya! It's very important in preparation for what's called fight or flight; meaning: 'do I have a better chance to survive if I run, or if I stay and fight?' It pumps blood more rapidly to the needed areas of the body, which helps the body prepare for either one of those actions. Natural fear is there to help you survive. So, it's normal and smart to be afraid of something that might be of danger to you, do you understand?"

They both nodded.

"Now listen up, because this is what you guys need to hear and understand."

He looked James square in the eyes, and then turned back to Kalan. Their faces were amber-colored, illuminated by the fire's glow. When he was sure that their attention was focused completely on him, Frank continued slowly and deliberately.

"What you do in that moment of fear, determines whether or not you become a hero, boys. Not letting fear stop you from doing what you know is right, makes you a hero. And you know what? The more you look fear right in the face and say, 'I'm not going to let you beat me!' the stronger you become. Trust me, guys, heroes can be just as afraid of something as anyone else. They're just regular people like you and me, but heroes do what they know is right and needs to be done, in spite of their fear."

Frank took a moment and watched as the boys thought over what he had just said. When he was absolutely sure that the boys understood, he twirled himself around and sank back into his chair, clasping his hands behind his head with a deep contented sigh and concluded, "Now that, gentlemen, is what I call a hero."

Chapter 11

Sheathed in Stone

"Look at that moon Dad," Kalan said as he pointed toward the heavens. "It's full, and you can really see the face."

"Oh good," Frank said as he looked up toward where his son was pointing. "I wanted to talk to you two about that tonight."

The forest canopy, and the occasional cloud, made it difficult to see the moon perfectly, but for the next few hours it would peek through every once in a while, shining a little extra light on the campsite and producing some eerie shadows.

"That's not just your ordinary full moon, Kalan. That moon is very special indeed. It's called a blue moon, and that means that it was the second full moon of the month. There's usually only one full moon in a month, so that in itself makes it a little unusual. But that moon is even more rare. It's a double blue moon, which means it's the second time this year that there have been two full moons in one month. That's pretty cool, you guys because that happens only about once every twenty years or so. And it just so happens to be on your birthday, Kalan."

"That is cool!" Kalan agreed.

"Speaking of your birthday, it's eleven forty five," Frank said, glancing at his watch. "Fifteen minutes till the big event."

"Oh yeah!" Kalan shouted. "What are we gonna do then, Dad...what's gonna happen?" Kalan was getting so excited he could barely stand it.

"You'll just have to wait and see, buddy," his dad said as he got up from his chair and started walking away.

"Where you going, Dad? Should I come with you?"

Frank had to laugh, knowing how eager his son was to find out what the heck was in store for him. "Nope, just hang in there, Kalan, and stay where you are. I'm going to get something out of the car. I'll be right back."

The boys turned and watched as Frank passed through the fire's circle of light and all but vanished into the shadows as he walked towards the car. The boys' attention was quickly diverted however by the sound of yet another faint howl, as it echoed through the woods across the lake.

"That's just spooky!" James said as he sat upright in his chair.

"It's only another coyote, James, that's all," Kalan replied trying to comfort his friend, and maybe himself just a little bit too.

"I don't care what it is," James snapped back. "It's still spooky!"

Minutes passed, and without Frank there to feed it, the fire ebbed and the boys felt the coolness of the night, mountain air for the first time. James pulled the hood of his yellow, USC Trojans sweatshirt up over his head to stop those little hairs on the back of his neck from standing up…it didn't help. Then, as the sound of a second howl, which seemed to grow louder as it skimmed its way across the surface of the lake toward their camp, reached an already tense James, he quickly realized that the cold had absolutely nothing to do with the little raised neck-hairs.

"Is it me, or is that thing getting closer, Kalan?"

But before Kalan could respond, James quickly pulled the hood down and turned his head to the side.

"What the heck was that?"

The boys sat quietly and listened. They could hear the crunching of dry pine needles, leaves and bark…footsteps. Someone or something was coming right toward them. They looked in the direction of the sound, but the moon hid behind a cloud making it too dark to see clearly. The boys knew that it couldn't be Frank, because they had watched him walk toward the car, which was parked up a ways and directly behind them as they faced the fire. Instead, these footsteps were coming from the tent area, which was to the right of the fire as you looked toward the lake, nowhere near the car.

"Dad!" A concerned Kalan called as he turned back toward the car.

Just then, from the direction of the mysterious footsteps, something emerged from the shadows, like Frankenstein's monster, and into the firelight.

"Yeah, Kalan?"

"AAHHH!" James yelled, falling back out of his chair and onto the ground as Kalan burst out of his chair.

Kalan then saw who it was.

"Geez, Dad, what are ya trying to do, scare us to death? I thought you went to the car!" Kalan said, a little annoyed with his father.

"I did," Frank laughed loudly. "But then I needed to get something from my bag, which was in the tent; is that okay with you guys?" He continued to chuckle. "Man oh man, what the heck is wrong with you two? I've never seen two kids more afraid of their own shadows. Snap out of it already" he said as he placed some articles down behind his chair.

Kalan began to laugh as he watched his best friend try to pull himself out of his chair, which had folded up on him. James couldn't help but laugh too, and once he managed to pick himself up off the ground and dust himself off, he repositioned his chair firmly in the dirt.

"Stay!" he yelled and pointed at the chair, as if training a puppy. They all laughed some more.

"Okay, first things first," Frank said as he lit a small candle with the end of the poking-stick he had been using on the fire. He then placed the candle on top of a large chocolate chip muffin, which was one of Kalan's favorites, and began to sing, "happy birthday to you…"

James immediately joined in, "happy birthday to you, happy birthday dear Kalan, happy birthday to you."

Frank leaned over and kissed the top of his son's head. "I love you Kalan. Happy birthday, buddy. Now make a wish, and blow out the candle," he said, handing the miniature cake to his son.

Kalan grabbed it and held it carefully in both hands. As he closed his eyes to make his wish, the wind suddenly began to stir.

"Must be one heck of a wish," Frank said with a smile, dismissing the gust even though it had been dead calm all evening.

While Kalan's eyes remained closed, the wind began to build, tousling his hair. As he drew in a deep breath of cool mountain air to blow out the candle, the wind blew even stronger. With his lungs full of air, Kalan opened his eyes and focused his attention on the target. At that moment a voice from deep within the child told him that something was just not right, but he was much too excited to stop and heed its warning and quickly dismissed it. Had he listened to the inner watchman, however, he surely would have noticed something very peculiar indeed. In all this blustery wind, the flame from the candle was perfectly still...not even the slightest flicker. As Kalan released his wish by easily extinguishing the candles' flame, some very strange things occurred simultaneously; the flames of the campfire suddenly erupted—shooting up three feet one second and returning to normal the next, while the cloud covered moon was again revealed and another howl shot across the lake, actually rippling the water as it advanced.

"Did you see that!" James exclaimed, pointing at the fire.

"Yeah, that was really something, wasn't it." Frank answered. "Must've been from the wind. Sometimes when it gusts, it feeds the fire with oxygen and makes it flare up like that. Look how low it is now though. I need to throw a couple more logs on there."

The boys looked at each other as Frank reached down for the wood. Kalan could tell that his friend was a little spooked, but now was just not the time for it. He had waited too long for this night to come, and nothing was going to dampen his excitement, nothing.

"Anyone want to split my chocolate chip muffin with me?"

"No thanks, buddy," his dad replied, tossing some fuel on the fire.

"I do!" James quickly answered, and just as quickly added, "did you hear that coyote?"

"Yeah, don't worry about it, James," Kalan said breaking the muffin in two. "It's not gonna hurt you, everything's fine," he added, handing his best friend the larger piece of cake.

As the boys took their seats and finished eating the muffin, Frank reached down behind his chair and grabbed something. As he came around to the front of the chair to sit down, the boys were able to see what it was that he held in his hands. It looked like an old cloth bag, which was tied closed at one end with a worn and frayed leather strap. Frank sat down in his chair and positioned himself just right. Taking great care, he then untied the sack and placed the leather bind in his shirt pocket. The boy's eyes widened as Frank reached into the timeworn pouch and pulled out a beautiful highly polished stone box. He gingerly placed it on top of the linen bag, which now lay across his lap. It looked as though it was made of some type of fossilized marble or granite, and by the way he handled it, the boys could tell that it was very heavy. The box was about twenty inches long, five inches wide and seven inches deep, and at first glance it appeared to be solid.

Frank placed his hands respectfully on top of the stone and closed his eyes for a moment as if to pray. "Before I open this, Kalan," Frank said, as he opened his eyes. "I need to tell you a story...a story that has been handed down in our family for many, many years."

Kalan just stared at the box. He knew now that not only was this artifact not solid, but also; whatever treasure was contained within its walls, had everything to do with him and his birthday. Though he seemed incredibly calm, you would've needed a box made of something much stronger than mere ancient, sacred stone to contain this boy's anticipation. The long awaited discovery of the family mystery was about to be revealed.

Chapter 12

The Great King Cathul

"Thousands of years ago, Kalan," Frank began, "one of your ancient ancestors was a great king named…"

"Really, Dad?"

"Yep, really," Frank replied with a smile. "At least that's how Papa told me the story goes. So anyway, this great king…"

"Thousands of years ago, Dad?" Kalan butted in again.

"Yes, Kalan," Frank said getting the least bit annoyed, "thousands of years ago. Now let me…"

"Wow, that would make him my great, great, great, great, great, great…"

"Knock it off, will ya!" His dad said putting a halt to his son's interruptions. "I don't know how many greats that would be, Kalan, but it's a lot, okay? Just let me tell you the story, will ya? If you keep interrupting me, we're gonna be here till the sun comes up."

James chuckled.

"Okay, Dad, sorry."

"So, where was I?" Frank asked, looking up toward the sky as if that's where he'd find his answer.

"A great king," Kalan and James answered at the same time.

"Oh, right, right…great king." Frank cleared his throat before he went on.

"Well, his name was Cathul, and he was not born to the throne, but was born a peasant under the evil rule of the cruel warlord, Braedon. Braedon gained the throne by heartlessly murdering his own father, King Bryant. Supposedly, Braedon started dabbling in the black arts as a child, and by his teens had already become some kind of wicked sorcerer, feared by all. After murdering his father, he ruled over the land with an iron fist. The ones that were closest to him, his court and guards, were said to be under a type of black spell, and would do anything for their evil king, even to the extent of torturing and murdering innocent people—including children."

"What a jerk," Kalan said under his breath as his father continued.

"With all their hearts and souls the villagers hated the ruthless king and prayed for his death. However, because of his incredible power, which oddly seemed only to increase as he aged, and his cruel and merciless nature, nobody dared disobey him or his laws, let alone rise up in arms against him. Except for one, that is.

"Cathul?" Kalan hoped.

"That's right, Kalan, Cathul...you're ancestor. Somehow he was able to defeat Braedon and his black magic, which in turn broke the spell the sorcerer had placed on those closest to him. The people, including those who were under Braedon's magic, were of course thrilled by what Cathul had done, and immediately and gladly appointed him to the throne. Cathul humbly accepted, and the people embraced him as their new king. He turned out to be a powerful and honest king who ruled over his fellow countrymen with wisdom, respect and kindness. In return he was greatly respected and dearly loved by all his subjects. With his life he promised the people that if or when he could no longer reign, he would make sure that only an honest, righteous man would take his place, and if at all possible that man would be his own blood, raised and taught by him from birth...his own first born son. And that is exactly what happened. The throne was passed down to Cathul's first born son, Cathmor."

Before continuing, Frank stopped just long enough to take another deep long breath, which was more for emphasis, than for any bodily need, and exhaled very slowly.

"Now..." he said tapping the stone lightly with his right index finger, "what is inside this box, Kalan, was supposedly handed down by Cathul himself, thousands of years ago, first to Cathmor, and then through the generations, father to first born son. The reason we're here tonight, Kalan, is because I promised, as you will, to do the same."

Kalan swallowed hard.

"Wow...awesome," James muttered, barely moving his lips.

The boy's just stared in awe at the pristine, stone relic, which Frank held on his lap with such care, wondering what it could possibly hold...dying to see inside. But before either boy could ask, Frank looked at Kalan and said, "Well, here we go, son."

Kalan's eyes widened even more and his face went flush as Frank held on firmly to one end of the stone with his left hand and carefully, ceremoniously slid the top of the box off with his right. As the lid was separated from its body, it released a sound so beautiful it could have come from an angel's harp—a delicate ring that hung in the air like the perfume from a fragrant rose. Taking care, Frank placed the lid of the box down on the ground next to his chair. He then took the thumb and index finger of both hands and gently pulled back the royal blue velvety fabric that covered the precious cargo, unveiling it for the first time in forty years. Not since Frank's dad took him camping and shared with him the tale of Cathul had the contents of this magical box seen the light of...night. Oh maybe a peek once in a while, through the years, but only that, a peek. For at least the last twenty-five years of Frank's watch, it had been neatly wrapped in its shroud, some type of fine ancient linen, which was spotted with a few drops of who-knows-who's blood, and securely tucked away in a floor safe in his walk-in bedroom closet. This was too cherished a treasure to be played with or even handled, outside the ritual that was about to take place on this sacred double blue moon night.

Chapter 13

The Sword of Torin

Kalan leaned forward in his chair to get a better look at what seemed to be giving off a faint glow. Was it just the reflection of the full moon off the highly polished stone, he wondered, or was the contents of the ancient box actually glowing? He took the briefest of moments and quicker than a blink—he didn't want to miss the great reveal—looked up at the sky, and back again. The glow was most certainly not coming from the moon, for it had crept behind yet another cloud, and was not to be seen. The light *was* coming from inside the box and now, Kalan's heart was beating faster than ever, as if he'd just finished running a mile. His dad grabbed the object when suddenly a surprised Kalan realized what it was. Strangely enough, he was very familiar with it.

"This sword," Frank said, lifting the weapon just above his head and slowly rotating it so both boys could see it clearly, "was a gift to Cathmor by another king." The reflection of the fire off the blade while Frank turned it, gleamed gold and landed on James' face, which immediately sent the boy into a strange trance. Kalan was way too involved in listening to the story and wondering what was to come, to notice what his best friend was going through. James was pretty much on his own right now, lost in some type of weird dream, while Frank continued.

"Supposedly, Cathmor had somehow saved the life of this king's son, so in return he gave Cathmor this sword, along with being forever indebted to him."

"Wow, that is so cool," Kalan whispered gazing at the sword. "Isn't it, James?"

But James didn't answer. Frank and Kalan looked over to see a zombie-like James just staring off into space.

"James?" Frank called softly. "Are you still with us, buddy?" he added with a chuckle.

But James said nothing. James was not there. Kalan felt another one of those—"something weird is happening here"—chills and leaned over to his friend.

"Hey, James!" Kalan yelled with a loud clap, snapping his friend back to reality.

"That looks just like mine!" James shouted still staring at the weapon, not yet completely back from his short but extremely eerie mental vacation. "That's just like mine," he repeated, but in a soft low voice, now waking fully from his strange dream.

"You alright, kiddo?" Frank asked with concern.

"Yeah…uh…I'm alright, why?" James answered not realizing what had just happened.

"Why? Because you're weirding me out, dude, that's why!" Kalan said shaking his head.

"Sorry," James said with a little smile "didn't mean to."

"No problem there, big guy. Now where were we?" Frank asked, eager to get on with the show.

"That sword looks just like mine," James reminded them in a soft calm voice.

"Really?" Frank answered.

"Yeah, Dad, it really does. It looks just like the one he's got, except yours is made of wood, James," Kalan said turning toward his best friend.

"Yeah, but everything else is the same," James pointed out.

It was true. It was almost identical to the one James had been using for at least the past two years to fight off their imaginary evil foes. It was a type of short sword. The blade, which was double edged, was about three or four inches wide near the hilt or handle, but the steel gradually tapered down to a sharp dagger-like point. The handle seemed to be made of some type of bone or ivory and metal. The blade and the handle combined were only about fifteen inches long; obviously a weapon used for close quarters fighting. Although the blade on the one James' grandfather had brought him back from Ireland, where his family was from, was made of wood, the design and materials of the handle were exactly the same. The only other difference the boys could see was the word TORIN, engraved on the blade of the one Frank now held.

"That's pretty unusual," Frank said. "I've seen similar ones in museums, but I've never seen another one quite like this one. You should be careful with it, James, it's probably very old and worth some money. Well anyway, tonight, Kalan, we're going to use this sword as it's been used in our family for many generations. We're going to use it to perform an oath."

"What's an oath, Dad?"

"Well, it's like a promise, Kalan," he said, carefully placing the dagger on the ground in front of him as he continued. "Usually when someone takes an oath, or promises to do something under oath, he's promising under God to fulfill the words he speaks. Like when someone goes in front of a judge in court, they promise, under oath, to tell the truth. If they break that promise and lie, they can be in a lot of trouble and even get sent to jail. In the old days when knights took an oath, they promised with their lives to uphold the laws of their code of chivalry."

"Like King Arthur and his knights of the round table?"

"Exactly like that, Kalan. If a knight broke a promise made under oath, they would be publicly humiliated and banished from the kingdom forever or maybe even put to death. Back then it was widely believed that if you broke a promise, you and your entire family could be cursed and horrible things would happen to you, so making a promise under oath is and always has been a very serious deal. Keeping your word is very important, Kalan, but I know you're already well aware of that," Frank said, pulling out an old parchment scroll and two pieces of paper from the stone box, as he placed it down on the ground to the right of his feet.

"What's that, Dad?"

"It's the oath, son. This is why we're here. This is what we are going to promise tonight to uphold with our lives, for as long as we live. The same oath that Cathul himself began, and swore to live by and keep alive thousands of years ago."

The wind picked up again and another howl swept across the lake, only this time, as it made its way to their side and into the camp, James could have sworn he heard the howl trail off into a whisper..."Kaaaalaaaann." Now, maybe it was just the wind he heard softly rustling the leaves in the trees, and his imagination was just getting the best of him; but then again, maybe not.

"What's the sword used for in the oath, Dad?" Kalan seemed a little puzzled.

"Well, Kalan, I was just getting to that. You know back in Cathul's time, whoever was taking an oath, would read the words of the oath out loud, and when they had finished, they would bind their word or promise with blood. Then after the ritual was completed, the newly initiated was given a quest or mission they needed to fulfill."

"Wait, wait, wait a second here. Back up just a little. Blood? Did you say blood?" Kalan asked, not quite sure where this conversation was headed, but certainly hoping it wasn't leading where he just thought it may be leading. "What d'ya mean blood? Whose blood?"

"Well, their blood, Kalan, whoever was taking the oath," Frank answered calmly, looking directly into his son's eyes. "What they would do back then, was to take a knife, or sword..." Frank leaned over and picked up the short sword from the ground below his chair in his right hand and showed it to Kalan before he continued, "...like this one, and make an incision across the palm of their dominant weapon hand..." Frank switched the sword over to his left hand and mimed slicing across his right palm before he continued, "...drawing blood. Then they would face each other and press their hands together so that their blood mixed with each other's as they stated their names and swore under God to never break the oath they just made."

Kalan scoffed, "Ha, that'd be the day huh, Dad?"

After a moment of uncomfortable silence, his dad answered straight-faced, "What do you mean, Kalan?"

"What do I mean?" Kalan snapped. "Well, obviously that doesn't happen any more, right?" He released a nervous chuckle. "I mean, that may have happened a long, long time ago, but not any more...right...Dad?"

Kalan just watched his dad's face; waiting, hoping it would change from that serious look, with which he was so familiar, to a smile or even a little smirk—anything that would let him know he was right, they don't do that anymore. He was pretty sure that after ten years, he knew his dad and his dad's wacky sense of humor well enough to know when he was pulling his leg, and right now was certainly one of those times; it had to be. Of course it was, how ridiculous of him to even think otherwise. His dad would never make him draw blood from his own little hand, for crying out loud. This was just another one of his dad's silly ploys to scare him and have a little fun with him, that's all. Surely this barbaric form of keeping promises was abandoned eons ago, by some of the smarter members of the family...right? Not that Kalan was afraid of slicing open the palm of his hand with an ancient, probably bacteria ridden blade, mind you...but come on already...it's 2006. I mean really, there's just got to be a more sanitary way of doing this whole blood oath thing without actually having to do the blood part…right?

"Well, you know what, Kalan?" Frank held up his right palm to reveal a two-inch long scar. "That is still the way it's done."

James let out a slight gasp.

Kalan had seen this mark on the inside of his dad's hand many, many times throughout the years, but, oddly enough, had never once thought to ask his father how he got it.

His jaw dropped and his eyes widened in disbelief. "You gotta be kidding me right, Dad?" Kalan asked, desperately hoping that this was just a dumb joke.

"I'm afraid not, son," Frank replied, "this always has been, and still is a blood oath."

"Neat," James muttered with a weird sort of excitement in his voice.

Kalan shot an icy glare at his friend as if to say, "what are you, some kind of a psycho or something?" then looked back at his dad whose face was still as serious as ever.

"Come on now, buddy, you're not afraid are you?" his dad asked. "Remember what we said about heroes."

From the corner of his eye, Kalan saw James look over at him, waiting for an answer.

"Heck no. I'm not afraid," he quickly decided. "If that's what you and all the others had to do, Dad, then that's what I'll do."

Frank smiled and nodded with approval. "That a boy, Kalan! I am really proud of you, son."

Kalan took a deep breath and smiled back. "Thanks, Dad." He loved hearing those words from his father, as any boy would, no matter what his age. It's amazing what just seven little words can do to a person's psyche, when they come from someone they love and admire. Those words actually gave the young warrior the strength and confidence he needed to face the challenge ahead.

"Are you ready, son?"

Kalan took a moment, then nodded. "I think so, Dad. I mean yes, I am."

"Okay then, buddy, here we go."

Chapter 14

Blood Oath

Frank stood up and carefully placed the sword on his chair where he could easily access it when the time was right, while holding the scroll and the other two pieces of parchment paper in his other hand.

"Stand up, Kalan, and face the fire," his dad ordered."

With his heart pounding, Kalan did as he was told.

It was as if the fire knew what was about to take place, and was joining in on the ancient ritual; because when Kalan stood up and faced it, out of nowhere, the flames of the fire surged suddenly, as they had before. This time, however, was very different. The heat from the flames was so incredibly intense, it forced James to quickly grab his chair and move away from the fire. When he turned back again to watch his friend continue with the ceremony, he saw something that absolutely amazed and confused him. The fire, which had now shot up about six feet into the air, seemed to be taking on a life of its own. Within the center of the flames, which by the way, didn't seem to be anywhere near too hot for Kalan or his dad, James saw the ghostly figure of a man begin to take shape. It never completely materialized, he could see right through it; it was more like an ethereal body, a spirit maybe. Was he dreaming, he wondered, or was this really happening? What happened next, though, made him question whether he was awake, even more. It was difficult for him to tell if they were made up of light or flames, but James watched the arms of this spectral being snake out from the fire and embrace his best friend. They lit up the boy's face with a beautiful yet eerie goldish-blue glow, which then started to flutter. Filled with a sense of wonder, he continued to watch Kalan when out of the blue an even more astonishing thing took place. Kalan's face began to assume the appearance of different people, young men and boys. It was as if Kalan's face were a movie screen, and the movie, entitled *Hundreds of Faces*, flickered across it in fast-forward. James immediately knew what was happening. He didn't know how he knew, nor did he care, he just knew that the faces he saw were those of Kalan's ancestors throughout the ages, who had taken the oath before him. They were there not only to witness and support their descendant, but also to reaffirm their promise, with him—through him; the oath bequeathed to all of them by their greatest grandfather, King Cathul, the figure in the fire. Were Kalan and Frank even aware of the strange series of events taking place around them, and to them, James wondered? If they were, no one would know it, because nothing was being said. They were just standing there, still as statues, in front of a terribly hot, blazing fire, totally unfazed. James was so engrossed in all the weird magical happenings, that when Frank finally did speak again, it startled him.

"Repeat after me, son." Frank unrolled the scroll and began to read aloud as the fire blazed before them.

Kalan listened carefully, and repeated every word his father spoke, without a flaw. James couldn't help but silently do the same.

"My life is sworn to valor.
My heart knows only virtue.

My blade defends the helpless.

My might protects the weak.

My words speak only truth.

My wrath undoes the wicked.

Right can never die.

Truth is never forgotten.

I promise with my life,

the spirit of this oath shall live on in my heart and soul,

'til evil is no more."

Frank lowered the scroll.

"Good, son. You did good," Frank said, nodding with a smile of approval. He rolled the scroll back up and placed it on the chair next to the sword. Anxiously anticipating the next step, the dreaded blood part, the boys watched Frank set the scroll down and reach for the sword. His thick, large hand hesitated for a moment, hovering just above the weapon.

James' eyes shifted quickly from the blade to Kalan and back again. *Is this really gonna happen?* he thought. *Is Mr. O'Shel actually gonna let my best friend slice the palm of his hand open with a sword? There's got to be some kind of law against something like this, right? This goes way past just being on the borderline of child abuse; you need some kind of special passport for this type of trip, don't you?*

As Frank grabbed the sword, Kalan inhaled deeply and with great determination. He was absolutely ready for what was about to take place. This is what he wanted more than anything in the world right now, to be a part of something so great, so important. To be able to join his father, and all those generations of O'Shel boys before them who had participated in this ceremony, in such an elite brotherhood.

Frank looked at his brave young son, smiled again, and then handed him one of the two parchment papers. Kalan quickly glanced at it. Written on the paper, was some kind of a poem. During his ten years of living, he had received more than enough birthday cards, holiday cards, post cards, notes and such, to easily be able to recognize his grandpa's writing. At the bottom of the paper, however he saw something else he recognized, but did not quite understand; two drops, or more like smears, of what he assumed was blood.

"What's this, Dad?" Kalan asked, without taking his eyes off the paper.

"That's the second part of the oath, son," Frank answered, "and that at the bottom, is blood," he added.

"Yeah, I thought that's what it might be. Whose blood, Dad?"

"Mine and Papa's."

Frank could tell that Kalan was waiting to hear some type of explanation, so he continued. "The poem on the paper was supposedly written by Cathul, as were the words we spoke just a minute ago," Frank said.

Kalan interrupted, "but I can tell that this paper is not very old, and this is Papa's handwriting, Dad."

"Well, you're absolutely right, son. But that's how it's been done for centuries. The scroll and the sword, Kalan, are ancient, but these…" he said referring to the papers they now held in their hands, "…are copies of Cathul's original oath, which his son Cathmor burned in the very first ceremonial fire. Papa copied the oath you hold, from a piece of paper that his dad copied from his dad, Papa's grandfather. He gave that to me on my tenth birthday around a fire very much like this one. You see, Kalan, tonight—your blood will be added to that piece of parchment as well, right next to Papa's and mine. Then, after we finish the oath, you will cast it into the fire, the same as Cathmor did many years ago. The one I have in my hand, I copied from that one. We will both add our blood to this one tonight, but you will keep it, until your son's tenth birthday. On that night, he will add his blood and toss it into the sacred fire. You will then take the hand written copy you will make, and add both your blood and your son's blood to that, and pass it down. Each time blood is drawn, and the oath is given and the paper burned, three generations of O'Shels are represented, and their promises bound. Do you understand?"

"Yes, sir," the boy answered, certain of what was next.

"Give me your hand, son," Frank said in a gentle but unwavering voice.

Kalan looked deep into his father's eyes, trying his best to draw from his strength, all the while desperately wishing he could be as fearless as him, his hero. Without hesitating, the boy reached his right hand out, palm up, and presented it willingly to his father. Frank took his son's hand from underneath and held it firmly in his as he raised the large dagger, positioning it just above the child's unblemished palm. Kalan couldn't help but squinch his face in anticipation of the cut, which Frank of course noticed.

"Do you trust me, Kalan?" Frank asked, sensing his son's anxiety.

Kalan's face immediately relaxed.

"Yes, sir."

James wanted to shout, "Stop! Don't do it!" However, he trusted Frank too, and something inside him told him that everything would be okay, or at least that's what he desperately wanted to believe.

"Then close your eyes, son," Frank said gripping the sword with intent.

With one deep breath, which he tightly held within his lungs, Kalan readied himself for the pain that he was sure was immediately to follow, and then, with his heart pounding, submitted to his father's request.

Marveling at his boy's bravery and strength, Frank smiled and repositioned the sword.

James was puzzled. He wasn't sure why Frank didn't just pull the weapon down, back and through Kalan's palm as he had envisioned it would go. Obviously that would be the easiest and quickest way to do it, because the blade was right there. Why was he taking so long? *Just do it if you're going to and get it over with already.* The waiting and anticipation was killing him.

Frank raised the blade, which was extremely sharp, so that it was perpendicular to Kalan's hand, and aligned the needle sharp point with the tip of the boy's middle finger. Then, as fast as lightening, pricked it, drawing blood. Without the slightest whimper, Kalan opened his eyes to see what his dad had done. The tip of his finger began to drip with his blood.

"Wait a minute, is that it?" Kalan asked with amazement.

"That's it, buddy," his dad answered. "You just showed a great amount of courage, son. The fact that you had every intention of going through with having your hand sliced open, shows just how incredibly brave you really are—and although that is exactly what they used to do years ago, it hasn't been done for generations."

"But what about the scar on your hand, Dad?"

"I had carpal tunnel surgery when you were less than a year old. I knew you wouldn't remember."

Kalan just smiled and shook his head. *Got me good this time,* he thought.

Although both boys were relieved, Kalan maybe a bit more, neither one could believe Kalan's dad had pulled one over on them.

There was actually a decent amount of blood, considering the tiny wound it was coming from. Needless to say, Kalan was extremely delighted that his dad didn't slice his hand open after all—but to one who sees the glass half full, a damaged hand could make it impossible to practice piano ever again! That would have been the upside as far as Kalan was concerned.

Frank released his son's hand and turned the blade to his own fingertip, and with the same speed and accuracy, pricked again.

"Ouch!" he cried. "Man, I hate that."

Kalan and James both chuckled.

"Remember what you said about heroes, Dad."

"Funny, Kalan. You're a very funny boy. Okay hurry, before it dries and I have to go through this again. Drop some blood on your paper, then on mine," Frank said as he wiped his finger on the parchment just below the oath.

Kalan dabbed some of his blood onto the paper in his hand and then reached over to add some to the other piece, which his dad held.

"Okay, now read along with me, Kalan, as I read the oath."

They both read aloud.

> "As blood flows from my flesh to fire,
> this oath I swear, my heart's desire;
> to honor family, faith and friends,
> and fight for good, 'til my life ends.
>
> From lowest bog to mountain peak,
> my sword shall help defend the weak.
> I'll slay the wicked without fear,
> and in their death not shed a tear.
>
> As my blood flows from flesh to flame,
> I challenge evil, know my name.
> Through darkest hours, God's light I'll keep,
> 'til every child can sweetly sleep."

Kalan felt a chill shoot through his entire body starting at the back of his neck as he spoke the last word.

"Okay, Kalan, toss it into the fire."

Kalan looked at the paper as if sad to see an old friend go, but crumpled it up nevertheless and threw it into the flames. There it was, thousands of years of history and tradition maintained and preserved. The fire flared one last time as if to seal the oath and then immediately subsided—dark once more.

James felt the cool night air caress his face once again. He had been so absorbed by the event, that he had totally forgotten how hot the fire had been on his face only moments before it settled, even at that distance. Then, in the dim light, another howl as again the moon began to take center stage. Except for the quest or mission, which would take place tomorrow, it was completed. The oath had been given, the promise made, too late to turn back now, even if they wanted to—even if they had any idea that there was a reason they should, which of course they didn't...not just yet.

Chapter 15

A Knight's First Quest

Well, you might as well have asked the sun not to set or a hawk not to fly, because that certainly would have been easier than getting two 10-year-old boys to fall asleep after such a day. Even as totally exhausted as they were, Frank still had to tell them to, "go to sleep!" at least three or four times after they had settled into their cozy sleeping bags for the night.

Too many weird and wonderful things had been jam packed into that one incredibly mysterious, exciting, and scary, yet fun-filled yesterday. Top a day like that off with nothing less than a blood oath at midnight, and you've got yourself a topic for conversation between two ten-year old boys that could last well into the wee hours of the morning, which of course is exactly what happened! Furthermore, as if that weren't enough, add to the mix the idea of a quest they must accomplish, and forget about it—*you* try to sleep.

Morning came and went without so much as a peep from the boys. Lifeless logs are what immediately come to mind. Frank let the boys sleep in, because he knew they'd be groggy, worthless and no fun at all if he hadn't. He didn't care though; to him, aside from Kalan's birthday and the oath, this trip was all about rest and relaxation. He gladly took the opportunity to settle down, undisturbed with a good book and a strong pot of campfire coffee, and read. Every once in a while, however, his focus would drift from the pages of the book only to land on some tender, faded memory. *What happened to the years,* he wondered. *How did they slip away, and so quickly? How is it possible that my little boy who used to be content with riding on top of my shoulders and falling asleep on my chest, is now already ten years old and I can barely pick him up anymore? Life can be so cruel,* he thought.

It seemed as though every time Frank took these occasional trips down Melancholy Lane, he would inevitably veer off down a path he'd rather not journey, it was much too painful. But just like a dog off the leash at its favorite "sniffing grounds" goes deaf to its owners commands, making it difficult to tell who's actually the boss; Frank's mind had its own agenda. Although reluctantly, he couldn't help but follow the traitor back to that heart wrenching day—the day his life turned upside down. *Karri, my love, where are you? How could you have just disappeared into thin air...gone without a trace? Did you really just walk out of my life of your own free will, or were you taken from us? And if you were taken, kidnapped, by who—or what?*

Frank hated even thinking about it anymore. What was the point? He knew that he'd never find an answer, for he'd been through this in his mind many, many times before. He wished he could just forget about that day all together, but he couldn't, it continued to haunt him through the years.

"Dad?" Kalan called from the tent, snapping a grateful Frank back to reality.

"Yeah, buddy?" Frank answered, closing his book.

"What time is it?" Kalan asked, while obviously stretching.

Frank was amazed when he looked at his watch and saw the time.

"Holy cow, it's almost noon!" Frank said, realizing that he'd been up and reading for almost five hours now. "Come on, guys, I'll make you some breakfast and then we'll get in a little fishing. What d'ya say?"

"What about my quest, Dad? I thought I had to go on a quest today." Kalan sounded a little disappointed. He hit James over the head with his pillow, and crawled out of the tent.

"Hey!" James pushed the pillow off his face, yawned and stretched.

"Don't worry about it, Kalan. I'll send you on a mission later. I already know what it's gonna be," Frank said, getting up and making his way over to the cooking area. "What do you want, boys, pancakes or bacon and eggs?"

"Bacon and eggs please!" Kalan shouted.

"Sounds great…please," James said as he climbed out of the tent.

"Coming right up."

It was surprising how quickly the next several hours passed, given how excited Kalan was about the quest his father was going to be sending him on before the day was done. *Good food*, he thought—

it always tastes better when you're camping for some reason—*and great fishing*—yep, time really does fly when you're having fun.

"Okay, Kalan, are you ready for your mission?" Frank asked as he closed his tackle box, and turned to make his way back up to the camp.

"What's it gonna be, Dad?" Kalan was dying to know.

"I'll meet you up at the picnic table, tell 'ya then," he replied.

The boys took the next few minutes collecting their equipment, all the while wondering what Kalan's dad had in store for them.

"Hurry up guys, before it gets too late!" Frank shouted from the campsite above.

As they reached the top of the hill, they could see Frank sitting at the picnic table, writing something down on a piece of paper.

"Put your poles and the tackle box down over there by the tent, and come over here and sit down for a second," his dad said without looking up from the paper.

"First off, what I'd like you two to do while I start dinner, is to take the path to the ranger station, which is less than fifteen minutes walk from here through the woods, even if you lollygag. Give them this piece of paper with our information on it. The campsite's already been paid for, so this is all they need. Put that in your pocket, Kalan, so you don't lose it. Do you understand?"

"Yes, sir."

"The next thing I want you to do is to walk right across the way from the ranger station to that little camp store. We've walked there a number of times before Kalan, so you know right where that is, correct?"

"Yes, sir," Kalan answered.

"Have them deliver two bundles of firewood to our campsite. That should only cost about twelve bucks. Here's twenty. I don't want you to lose this either so put this in your pocket too, Kalan. Do you have any questions so far?"

"Yes sir," Kalan replied as he folded the twenty-dollar bill, placed it securely in his pocket, and then subtly nudged James without his father's detection.

At that moment, James became acutely aware of where his cohort was so cleverly leading his father in this strategic exchange. He could sense Kalan's well-devised plan. Kalan's genius was beginning to show. Was it too obvious? He hoped not. The suspense was too much for James to bear, and as the slightest of smirks began to emerge on his face, Kalan skillfully guided his father in for the kill.

"What should we do with the money that's left over?" Kalan so smoothly asked.

To the boys, the next few seconds seemed as if time stood still before Kalan's dad finally reacted with a chuckle and said, "whatever's left over, you boys can either split 50/50 and keep, or you can use it to buy whatever you want at the store. It's up to you, okay?"

"Yes, sir!" they cried out in unison.

That was just way too easy, James thought. *His father never even had a chance.*

As James let out a sigh of relief, Kalan turned to him with a smile and a raised eyebrow as if to say, *am I good, or what?*

"Now, I know I'm giving you guys a little bit of responsibility here," his father continued, "but I also know you two can handle it with no problem. I'm letting you test your wings, so to speak, but I want you guys to listen to me and be smart. It's important that you stay on the path. Do you understand? Don't be wandering all over the place."

They both nodded.

"It's gonna get dark around eight o'clock tonight, so I want you guys to be back here by seven. It's just after six now," he said looking at his watch. "That gives you more than enough time to walk there, take care of business, shop around a little bit and walk back. Keep an eye on your watch, Kalan, and take this little flashlight and whistle with you. Now what's the rule about the whistle, Kalan?" his dad asked dangling it in front of the boy 'til the proper answer was given.

"Don't blow it unless it's an emergency," he quickly answered.

"That's right," his dad asserted pointing his finger at his son just for emphasis.

"Can we take our swords with us, just in case?"

"In case of what?" Frank inquired.

"I don't know. You always say that it's good to be prepared, Dad."

"Yeah, maybe we'll have to kill a couple dragons on the way," James said.

"Or fight off some black knight or something," Kalan added.

"Sure, go ahead," his dad said with a smile. "But I don't want you guys to get carried away and lose track of time. Even now it's gonna be quite a bit darker on the path through the woods than it is here at the campsite, so just be aware of what's going on around you and be careful, understand?"

"Yes sir," they both answered.

"No problem, Dad," Kalan added.

"Okay then, go get your swords and take off."

The boys raced each other to the tent, and grabbed their swords. As they ran from the tent past the picnic table Kalan shouted, "I love you, Dad."

"I love you more," Frank replied.

"I love you just as much!" Kalan yelled back as he and his buddy hit the path leading into the forest.

"Not possible!" his dad shouted as the two disappeared into the woods.

Little did the boys know what lie waiting ahead, what the darkness beyond the shadows had in store for them...their quest had just begun.

Chapter 16

When Day Dreams Come True

As the boys walked farther and farther away from the safety of the camp and the watchful eye of Kalan's father, and deeper into the cool darkening forest realm, James' pace began to slow, until he came to a halt several feet behind Kalan. As soon as Kalan realized his friend was lagging so far behind, he turned to see a statue-like James just starring at the ground.

"Come on, James, what are 'ya doing?"

"Hey, Kalan," James said in a trembling whisper, "remember the rainbow with a tail in our daydream?"

Kalan thought for a few seconds before answering, "yes."

"Those were the rainbow trouts we caught today," James said as if piecing together a mysterious puzzle.

Bewildered but intrigued by his theory, Kalan slowly stepped closer to his companion.

"And the black cloud; do you remember that in our dream?" James asked as he lifted his eyes to meet Kalan's.

"Uh huh," Kalan quietly confirmed.

"It's coming true, Kalan. Our daydream is coming true!"

Several moments passed while Kalan carefully pondered his friend's belief. "Yeah…" acknowledged a hypnotized Kalan, "…but wha-what about the wo-wolf and the owl?" Kalan stuttered, swallowing hard. "That can't come true, can it? I don't want that to come true."

The boys looked at each other as their fear began to build.

"Maybe we should turn back, Kalan. It's not too late. We could just tell your dad that we got lost or something."

"No!" Kalan demanded, determined to see this thing through. "We were given a quest, James, and we have to complete it. Don't you get it? If we don't, we're not knights. We're just a couple little sissy scaredy-cats!"

A few thoughtful moments passed before James spoke. "I won't tell anyone if you don't," he said, hoping Kalan would come to his senses.

"No James! *Real* knights wouldn't be afraid of walking in the woods," Kalan said, determined to convince his friend and himself that there was nothing to fear. "We're only talking about some stupid daydream anyway. It's not real!" Then, decisively he drew his plastic sword from his belt, and held it firmly and courageously in front of James and dared, "I'm gonna keep going, James…are you with me or not?"

Without looking or saying a word, James pulled his sword from his belt with one swift motion and bravely answered his friend's challenge with a resounding "donk" that echoed throughout the forest; the unmistakable sound of plastic hitting plastic. The gauntlet had indeed been thrown down: knights against the evildoers. Whatever lay ahead waiting in the shadows to attack, best be prepared for a fight. For these young, fearless warriors would not easily be defeated. The quest was to continue.

Chapter 17

From Knight to Knave

With every young, vibrant breath and each passing step of their journey, the boys grew more and more confident and at ease. They actually began to have fun again, while fighting off their imaginary foes. Weep not for the souls of those imaginary, villainous cutthroats that carelessly crossed their path. What pathetic dolts they were, to believe that disguising themselves as low hanging branches could ever fool these skillful boy warriors. One by one these make-believe ne'er-do-wells would rise up in arms against the duo, only to be unyieldingly cut down by one or both of the fearless knights' mighty blades.

As they reached just about halfway point of their trek, they heard something very real off to the right of the trail that startled them. It sounded as if a rock had been thrown into the brush. Then it sounded more like someone, or perhaps something, was running through the bushes not far from where they were walking. That's all that was needed for the boys' imagination to take control of the situation and plunge them into the depths of darkness without even so much as another step.

"Did you hear that, Kalan? What was that?"

They stood frozen in their tracks, with their heads slightly cocked trying to determine just what it was that pierced through the natural lull of the forest's sweet song.

"I don't know, James, probably just some pine cones falling from a tree. Come on," he urged his friend. "Let's just keep walking."

So onward they pressed. The boys' gait quickened as their awareness heightened. Within moments they heard another noise that demanded their immediate attention, as well as their last bit of nerve.

How little it takes for a mood to change, or a warrior's courage to waver; the sounds of the wind through the trees, or a pine cone falling to the leaf-laden forest floor below...a harsh word from a loved one. It's amazing, and so sad, how the smallest amount of fear and self-doubt can send even the strongest of soldiers crashing to their knees. From knight to knave in less time than it is possible to measure.

The boys were frightened half to death. They had both played enough sports to know that unmistakable sound...the sound of someone running up from behind you. Only this time, it wasn't some pint-sized soccer-playing rival that was breathing down their necks. Nor was it the least bit interested in team sports. Right now, something very large and very scary was running up from behind them on the path, and...it was gaining on them.

Without missing a stride, Kalan turned his head around just in time to see a huge, dark figure leap into the woods off to the left of the path.

"Run, James run!" Kalan cried, as he sprinted faster than he ever imagined he could. "Don't look back, James, just run...RUUUN!"

As the boys' hearts pounded, adrenaline surged through their bloodstream, enabling their little legs to carry them to speeds they had only dreamed of before.

Suddenly, they heard an unearthly howl from off to the left of the path where they were running. As they turned their heads in the direction of the freakish wail, all they could see in the dim forest light was the dense thicket and brush that lined the forest path, moving at the same pace at which they were running. Whatever it was had already caught up with the boys and was cutting through the bushes with ease, parallel and even with them some fifteen yards away. It was as though this creature was taunting them, testing them. Just when the boys thought they couldn't be any more unnerved, the beast began to let out a deep...rhythmic...demonic grunt with every stride it took.

"Kalan, I'm scared!"

"Me too, but just keep running, James, as fast as you can!" Kalan shouted to his friend between breaths.

Kalan glanced again to the left of the path, and could tell by the movement of the bushes that the monster was now sprinting ahead of the boys as if to cut them off at the pass.

A little further up the way was a clearing. Kalan could see the golden, amber-colored rays of the afternoon sun shining down and illuminating the mouth of the trail, but he could also sense the creature starting to angle towards them to bring an end to this game. He was sure it was about to attack!

"Run, James, faster! We're almost there. RUUUUN!"

"AAAHHHRR!" they screamed, with a final sprint to safety. As they lunged for their freedom, they felt, in every fiber of their being, the creature lunge for them. As they burst into the opening, and narrowly escaped into the sun, the boys saw a huge shadow pass over them and enter the woods. It seemed to bring with it a gust of wind so strong, it rustled the treetops and the shrubbery below. Then a "THUD," just as the creature let out a blood-curdling scream, which seemed to quickly fade into the depths of the forest while simultaneously rising above it.

Panting heavily, the boys stopped and turned towards the retreating sound.

"What just happened, Kalan? What the heck was that?" James asked, desperately trying to catch his breath.

"I don't know," answered Kalan, also breathless, but very relieved.

"I wasn't sure we were going to make it, but we did, and we're okay. We're okay, James." Kalan swallowed hard, then continued, "boy, did that thing give me the heebie-jeebies. I'm never going back in there again, that's for sure. No way! We'll walk along the road on our way back to the campsite," he demanded.

"That sounds good to me," James replied.

A few minutes passed as they caught their breath.

"Man, Kalan, I can't believe how fast we were running. It felt like we were flying."

"Yeah, I know. I don't think my feet were even touching the ground!" Kalan said, as he turned towards James and they both began to laugh.

At that moment James remembered what Kalan had around his neck that his dad had given him in case of an emergency. "How come you didn't blow the whistle, Kalan? You should have blown the whistle."

Kalan grabbed it and held it tightly in his hand. "Are you kidding me? I forgot I even had it. I was so scared I didn't even think about it."

Exhausted and relieved, the boys fell to their knees and again started laughing, breaking the tension.

Chapter 18

R. Goodfellow, Park Ranger

Sometimes I meet them as a man;
sometimes an ox, sometimes a hound;
into a horse I turn me can,
to trip and trot about them round.
But if to ride
my back they stride,
more swift than wind away I go;
over hedge and lands,
through pools and ponds,
I whirry, laughing, ho, ho, ho!

When lads and lasses merry be
with food and beverages so fine,
unseen by all the company,
I eat their cakes and sip their wine;
and to make sport,
I fart and snort,
and out the candles I do blow;
The maids I kiss,
they shriek, "Who's this?"

I answer not, but ho, ho, ho!

_____

Some call him Robin Goodfellow,
Hobgoblin or mad Crisp,
and some again do term him often,
by name of Will the Wisp;
But call him by what name you wish,
I have studied on my pillow,
I think the best name he deserves
is Robin the Good Fellow.

The Mad Merry Pranks of Robin Goodfellow
Ben Jonson 1628

As the boys continued their laughing jag, they heard another "THUD" and then immediately, Kalan felt something grab his back and shoulder from behind.

He bolted to his feet screaming, "AAHHHH!!" which in turn scared the dickens out of James, who then jumped to his feet and joined in.

They quickly turned to see a stilt-legged, thin-cheeked, gawky looking man picking himself up from the ground, brushing himself off, and laughing, a peculiar little laugh. He stood towering over them. He was in a uniform, and the reflection from the sun off his badge momentarily blinded James.

Kalan looked at the engraved nametag above the badge, which read, 'R. Goodfellow'.

The man began to speak in a funny, high-pitched voice that seemed to come from somewhere between his nose and the back of his throat. "Easy boys," and then that funny laugh again, a weird, eerie kind of chuckle; very freaky. "My goodness, take it easy, you have nothing to fear," he said. "My name's Robin. I'm the ranger here. I heard a scream, so I rushed out to see if someone was hurt. You boys okay?"

Kalan was immediately drawn to the man's face, particularly his glasses. The lenses were so thick they resembled the bottoms of coke bottles as he squinted through them. His eyes looked like black little BBs through the dense magnifiers. Kalan wondered how the man could even see where he was going in the bright day sun, let alone make his way through the dimly lit forest, if he needed to, as a ranger.

The boys really didn't mean to be rude, nor would they ever intentionally make fun of someone. They knew better than to do that. However, the combination of the relief they felt from escaping the creature, and the surprise of running into Ranger Robin, made for a perfect involuntary, reflexive reaction. As inappropriate as it may have been, they just looked at each other and started to laugh again.

"Yes sir, we're fine now," Kalan answered, doing his best to stifle his giggling and be respectful. "We just walked through the woods from our campsite and got a little scared, that's all."

"Yeah, something was chasing us!" James exclaimed.

Kalan's attention was unexpectedly drawn down to the ground around the ranger's feet; there he noticed something totally out of the ordinary, very strange indeed. The ranger was shoeless, which

Kalan thought was very unusual, to say the least. However, much odder still, were the ranger's feet. They were extremely hairy, downright furry in fact, with long claw-like nails. It sent a cold chill down Kalan's spine, and he desperately wanted to point this out to his best friend, but there was just no way of doing that without the ranger knowing, so instead, he wisely chose to remain silent.

"Really? Something was chasing you, huh? Well, that's not good, is it?" The ranger said with another weird laugh as he swooped his head down placing his face within inches away from James' face. "What did it look like, hmmmm?" the ranger asked with a devilish little smirk. His breath was horrendous.

"We don't know," James said, taking a slow step back away from the stench, not quite sure whether to be afraid of this strange man, or laugh. "We didn't really get a good look at it, it's so much darker in there," he said pointing towards the forest.

"Oh, yes you're right, it is darker in there...much darker I'm sure," the ranger replied in a low, edgy type of whisper, much different from what he sounded like just a moment ago. "Well, you know the forest can be a very scary place if you're not used to it...like me. Yes, verrrry scary indeed. There are lots of shadows and different sounds that can play tricks on you, aren't there; yes there are. You know there's an old Indian legend that tells of creatures, called shape shifters that used to inhabit these woods. Shape shifters, you know what they can do? They can turn themselves into anything they desire; a goat, a frog, a butterfly or even another man or a woman—anything. But of course, like I said, that's just legend. You can't be chased by something that doesn't even exist, now can you?" Then suddenly, out of the blue he asked, "You wouldn't happen to have any milk or cream with you that I could have, would you? I do so love milk and cream, I do."

"Milk or cream?" a puzzled Kalan asked turning towards an even more puzzled James.

"Oh yes, milk or cream, that would be nice, thank you."

Kalan was beginning to get just a little freaked out by the odd behavior of good old Ranger Robin, and something inside the boy told him not to trust this man, but he was too confused to figure out whether he should stay and be respectful, or heed his intuition and turn and run. His anxiety grew.

"Gee…uh, no sir, we don't have any…milk or cream on us. Sorry."

Kalan just couldn't figure this guy out. *Maybe he's acting strange because he thinks we're just a couple of punks that are lying to him and wasting his time or something. Yeah, that's probably it,* he thought. *He's just toying with us to teach us a stupid lesson…of some kind.* After all, if Kalan and James were having a hard time believing what had just happened to them in the woods, how could they expect an adult, you know someone with much less imagination, to believe?

Well, whatever it was, the bizarre behavior continued.

"Awe, don't feel embarrassed or…stupid, kids, lots of little people your age get scared and panicky out here in the wooooods!" he said, tripping, yet again, over another rock and falling to the ground. Only this time he didn't even bother to pick himself up and brush himself off. Instead he just lay there on the ground, on his back, nonchalantly clasping his hands behind his head and gazing up at the sky. "I remember one little boy that got chased back to his campsite by a squirrel," he added, before pausing momentarily to adjust his goggles and scratch his boney butt. "I think he peed in his pants too, if I remember correctly," he said with a huge spooky smile. "Yeah, yeah I'm almost sure he did." All of a sudden he jumped to his feet with the skill of an Olympic gymnast, which totally startled the boys, swooped his head down again, turned his mole-eyed face to them and said, "at least you kids didn't pee in your pants, am I right, hmmm?" Then he just stared at the boys with those crazy thick glasses, and black beady eyes until they answered.

Man oh man, talk about an uncomfortable moment.

"Right," Kalan finally uttered, as he nudged James.

"Yeah...yeah, that's right," James agreed, every bit as baffled as Kalan.

Yes, it was more than apparent to the boys that this man was not only nuttier than a fruitcake, he wasn't to be trusted. Nor was he inclined to search the woods for a mysterious creature, they were sure of that. In fact, by now the boys were thinking that good old Ranger Goodfellow was much more mysterious and a whole lot weirder and scarier than whatever it was that chased them through the forest in the first place. As far as Kalan and James were concerned, they were probably better off, and safer, if they just parted company now.

Therefore, although extremely reluctant to do so, Kalan gave the ranger the paper with the reservation information on it as his dad requested and turned to James, "let's get the heck out of here," he whispered.

Without hesitation, James nodded in agreement.

"Well, uh…thanks a lot for, uh…thanks!" Kalan stammered as they turned to continue on their quest.

"Oh boys!" the ranger shouted.

They didn't want to, but they turned around just the same, to see Ranger 'Weird-fellow' slowly creeping towards them with the scariest looking smile the boys had ever seen. He was also much shorter than he was just a moment ago. To top it all off, his glasses were now gone revealing crazy looking eyes that were wide open and bright yellow.

"What the…" Kalan was shocked. "How can that be?"

The chill that shot up the back of James' spine was so strong; it just about knocked him off his feet.

"Be careful walking through the forest on your way back home, boys," the strange man added in yet another different and eerie voice. "Never know who or what you might run into." Then, that crazy, freakish laugh again.

"Let's go James, now!" Kalan shouted. The boys turned and ran as fast as they could. Kalan looked over his shoulder, and saw this disturbing little man dancing round in circles. Without breaking stride, Kalan turned back to James and shouted, "James, look! Look at that guy!"

But, when James turned to see what his friend was referring to, the man was gone, vanished. James stopped dead in his tracks and told Kalan.

Kalan stopped and turned around, and to his amazement, no one was there.

"That sure as heck was no Ranger!" James exclaimed as he tried to catch his breath.

"No, sure wasn't, but, if he wasn't a ranger, then what the heck was he?" Kalan asked.

They looked at each other for a second and then back to the empty field.

"Are we nuts or something?" Kalan asked, frustrated and confused. "I mean, what's going on anyway. These past few days have been the weirdest days in my life, by far."

"Yeah, I'll say." James thought for a moment. "Hey, you know what? Maybe, just maybe it has something to do with your birthday."

"My birthday? What are you talking about? What could all that's been happening to us in the last couple days, possibly have to do with my birthday?"

James shrugged his shoulders. "I don't know. It just seems kind of strange that all these crazy things are taking place at the same time as your birthday and the oath and the double blue moon and everything."

Kalan thought about it. There was just no way around it. It seemed much too coincidental. "Yeah, you're right," he agreed.

"You know, I didn't want to say anything because I thought you might think I was crazy or day-dreaming or something," James continued, "but, you know when you were taking the oath last night?" He looked over to Kalan to make sure he was following this.

"Yeah?" Kalan asked, waiting to hear more.

"A lot of really weird stuff was happening."

"What do you mean, James, like what?"

"Well, for one thing, now don't laugh, but I saw some guy standing in the middle of the fire. I know that sounds stupid, but I did. I know what I saw. I think maybe it was the ghost of King Cathul." James stared at his best friend and waited for some kind of response.

"Wow, I thought I was imagining that guy in the fire," Kalan replied, "but you saw him too. He was really there. You know, I kept going in and out of some kind of trance or something. I felt like I was standing there, right next to the fire with my dad one minute, and then in some far away place the next. Yeah, I'm sure it was King Cathul too. What else, James?"

"Well," James tried to think of the best way to describe the odd events of last night to his best friend. "Your face started to change…into other faces, kind of—I don't know, it's hard to explain, but I saw it. I think those other faces were all the guys in your family, you know, from the past, that took the oath before."

Kalan was silent, thinking about what had just been said.

"And how come you and your dad could stand right next to the fire when it was so hot, and I had to move back, like five feet? How was that possible, huh?"

"I don't know, James," Kalan said in a soft voice, a bit stunned.

"It was actually really cool though, Kalan. I mean, I don't get it, but it was really cool."

James let it all sink in for a moment before he placed his hand on his friend's shoulder, looked him in the eye and said, "Come on, Knight-buddy. Let's finish our quest. We got some fire wood and candy to buy before we get back to the campsite, I mean the castle."

That brought a smile to Kalan's face. "Yeah, let's go. Last one to the store's a monkey butt!" Kalan said, as they raced away.

Inside the store they both eagerly searched the shelves for just the right thing to spend their money on. There was so much to choose from; toys of all kinds, candy, fishing lures, snacks and even some kites. The kites were great but a little too expensive. After much deliberation, they figured they had just enough money for both of them to buy these really neat cap guns, and maybe a candy bar or two.

"Let's hurry up, and pay for everything, so we can get back to camp before it gets dark," Kalan said.

"What time is it?" James asked.

"It's"...Kalan reached for his watch...but it was gone.

Chapter 19

The Last of King Arthur's Knights

The beautiful pocket watch, with the colorful enameled picture of a soaring eagle on the case that his grandpa had given him for his birthday, was gone. Kalan looked at the watch chain, and saw that the swivel at the end of the chain was broken.

"Oh no!" he cried. "You gotta be kidding me! I can't believe this, James. It's gone! The watch that Papa gave me is gone! You have to help me find it, James," Kalan pleaded. "I need to find it, or my dad's gonna kill me."

With the help of his friend, he frantically began to search the floor and the surrounding area outside of the store, but they could find nothing. They began to backtrack, all the while fearing the worst. They searched all along the road they had to cross to get to the store…nothing. They looked up and down and all around the path that led back to the ranger station, and now they stood at the edge of the ever-darkening forest…nothing.

"I know what happened!" Kalan shouted. "We both know where I lost it! We both know what I have to do!"

Kalan was so frustrated and frightened at the prospect of having to go back into the woods to retrieve the prized gift, he was absolutely beside himself. But he knew there was no other way. He knew he could not go back to the camp without the watch. How could he be so irresponsible? How could he not know when the watch fell? What would his dad think? How could he ever look his grandpa in the face again if he didn't even try to find it?

He paced back and forth for several minutes, trying to muster the courage he knew he would need to pull this off. With each step he took, the fear grew inside him. Without a whimper the tears began to stream down his face. The fear became so great and so strong, it literally paralyzed the child. As Kalan stood there motionless, staring at the ground with his little body trembling and the fear filling him completely, something strange began to happen to him.

James watched in silent awe as his friend's incredible transformation began to unfold. Kalan's body began to change right before his very eyes. His shoulders and head, which were hunched over in defeat just moments before, began to slowly rotate backward and upward towards the heavens. James was sure Kalan was growing taller.

In less than a second, every muscle in his face relaxed and his eyes glazed over and became fixed on something in the distance that James could not see. His brows began to furrow and his feet, as if strategically guided by some outside force, smoothly and deliberately maneuvered themselves into a stance so solid and so strong, it could have supported even the largest man. His hands and fingers prepared themselves for battle by first spreading open wide, as if gathering energy and power from the air and space around them, and then clenching themselves tightly into fists.

Within seconds after it had begun, the change was complete, and James could hardly believe that it was his friend, Kalan, who stood before him. It would have been easy for anyone to see, by the difference in his companion, that a stronger, less tolerant emotion had suddenly appeared on the scene. Anger had just arrived fashionably late, and was ready to party. But Anger did not come alone, and quickly called upon his older and much more violently explosive brother Rage to help remove any uninvited riffraff—fear—from Kalan's inner sanctum. Fear was no longer welcome here and had nowhere to hide, no place to live. You could say that it tucked its weasely, hairless tail between its scrawny little legs and went crying home to mommy, with the bitter taste of defeat heavy on its tongue.

"Why should I be afraid of going into the woods? I have just as much right there as any other creature!" Kalan demanded. "I need to find the watch that Papa gave me, and nothing's gonna stop me from doing that. Do you hear me? NOTHING!" he shouted with the greatest of determination.

The little peach-fuzz hairs on the back of James' neck stood up as he watched Kalan explode with confidence and power. It was something he'd never witnessed before…anywhere…from anyone. It was like some great warrior had moved into Kalan's little body and completely taken over, and wasn't about to put up with anything from anybody!

If Arthur himself stood before this boy, would he not immediately understand his valiant character? Would he not see his own spirit mirrored in this child's eyes, and surely Knight him? For he too was just a boy endearingly called "Toad" when first taken under his mentor Merlin's wing to be taught and made king.

Yes, indeed he would, without hesitation. For the courage and honor this lad displayed was every bit as great as was the bravest of men that King Arthur had ever knighted throughout his reign in Camelot. The great wizard, Merlin, had wisely taught Toad that the spirit of a true knight lies in the heart and soul of a man, or in this case a boy, and is borne out of his actions. Knightly courage knows, nor cares, nothing of years or size.

Kalan exhaled a deep, powerful breath. Then, as he calmly pulled his sword from his belt, more than ready to face whatever his quest may bring, a vision slowly materialized before him. James looked on with astonishment, blinking rapidly as if he could wash away this mythical mirage from his eyes. But he could not, and he soon realized whom now stood before them. It was none other than Kalan's legendary hero, King Arthur, who looked down and smiled proudly at Kalan. Then reaching out with his great sword Excaliber, which he had pulled from the stone as a child to be made The Boy King, and touched him thrice; once to the left shoulder, then slowly and deliberately to the right. Then finally, the King brought the great blade down to rest softly upon the young man's crown.

The fabled weapon seemed to glow with its own inner radiance and awareness, as Arthur spoke. "I knight thee," the ghostly king whispered to the boy, while James leaned forward straining to hear the words. "...Sir Kalan of Dragonfly's Meadow," he finished as he raised Excaliber with a nod then slowly disappeared.

The last of King Arthur's knights turned slowly towards James, and looked him directly in the eyes. "I'm going back in there to get my watch, James," he stated with ease and confidence...and if I have to, I'm gonna kick me some creature butt."

Chapter 20

A Brave Decision

Kalan turned and began to make his way back into the mysterious, dark unknown.

Impressed with his friend's unbelievable courage, James watched, in awe. Kalan hadn't taken ten steps into the bewitched forest before reality dawned on James.

"Hey, wait a minute...what about me?" he shouted, quite surprised and a little aggravated with how easily Kalan could abandon him. "What the heck am I supposed to do?"

"Just follow the road back to the campsite, James. You'll be alright there, I'm sure of it," Kalan said, turning again towards the forest. "I need to do this," he added, as he took yet another step closer to the world without light.

"Wait, just wait a second, will ya?" James immediately stopped Kalan in his tracks again. "I may be all right, but how about you? I can't just let you go back in there by yourself, knowing what might be waiting for you there. I wouldn't be much of a friend, or a knight, if I did." James took a deep breath, looked Kalan straight in the eyes and said, "a knight would help, so I'm going with you. That's what friends are for."

Kalan smiled at James, understanding quite well the sacrifice his friend was making and the courage it took to make it.

"I have no idea what it is we're up against, James. I don't know what will happen to us."

"I do," James replied, as his chest filled and lifted with confidence. "We're gonna find your watch Kalan, and if we have to…we're gonna kick some creature butt!"

Chapter 21

The Perfect Stone

With that the two warriors unsheathed their blades and firmly crossed them into each other with a hero's resolve. Maybe it was just their imagination, or possibly their hearts were pounding so loudly, their ears were fooled, but when their blades hit this time, it wasn't the sound of plastic *donking* plastic; it was the thunderous resound of cold, hard steel clanging. The sound echoed through the forest.

Without a word they turned and made their way back into the woods. It seemed so much darker than before; and within only a few minutes time, Kalan realized something else was very different, and very wrong.

"What's the matter, Kalan? Why are you stopping?"

"Do you hear that, James?" Kalan asked, as he closed his eyes to focus all of his attention on one sense alone.

"I don't hear anything, Kalan."

"Yeah, exactly...me neither," Kalan said, as he cocked his head in different directions and angles as if fine-tuning a radar dish in search of a better signal. "Not one little thing."

Deafening, tomblike silence lay hold on the forest's song. No birds chirped or crickets called. No leaves floated dreamily down from the trees above to settle gently upon the floor below. Even the wind stopped whispering her sweet secrets to the trees. Nothing was heard, save the slowly crescendoing beat of two brave, but unseasoned hearts.

Just at the moment when stillness peaked, the calm was shattered as the silencer spoke. "Haaaoooooowww," a not so distant, disapproving howl rolled through the forest, as if to say, *you will not get away from me this time*, and it chilled the boys to the bone.

"Help me find the perfect stone, James," Kalan urged, as he directed his focus to the path below.

"Perfect stone? What are you talking about, Kalan?"

As Kalan kicked leaves to the side in search of ammunition, he revealed his slingshot, which was hidden in the back pocket of his blue jeans under his sweatshirt.

"What are you gonna do with that?"

"I need a stone, James...just help me find a stone!" he demanded. "We don't have time to..."

Before he could finish his sentence, another low eerie howl swelled through the woods. Only this time it was much closer. Whatever it was, it was advancing.

"Here's one!" Kalan shouted, holding up an almost perfectly round specimen.

"Hold this, James…hurry!" He pushed his sword toward his friend, freeing his other hand.

In the twinkling of an eye, Kalan unfolded his Black Widow slingshot, quickly slipped his hand into the wrist support, wrapped his fingers firmly around the molded grip and carefully loaded the stone, making sure to center it perfectly within the leather pouch. As he finished his preparation, their attention was abruptly drawn to a bush not twenty yards from where they stood. It moved…ever so slightly. Kalan was taking no chances. With his left arm fully extended and his right hand holding the projectile firmly between his thumb and index finger, he pulled back on the latex power band with all his might, stretching it to its limit, until the pouch barely touched his cheek just below his right eye. Kalan aimed at the unseen, soon to be unfortunate, creature that caused this shrubbery to stir. He was ready to fire. As he held this pose with all his strength his nervous little hand quivered from the tension of the rubber bands, and lightly tapped his face.

Kalan flashed back to a time when he and his father took the slingshot out to the desert to do some target shooting. He was amazed at how powerful it was and the damage it caused as he watched the steel shot rip through a tin can. "Just imagine if that were an animal, son. It wouldn't stand a chance. It's not a toy, Kalan, you could kill someone with this. You need to be very, very careful where you aim it. You don't want to hurt anyone or anything." His dad's words kept echoing through his mind.

"What are you waiting for, Kalan? Shoot!" James was terrified.

"I'm afraid to," he answered, as his hand tapped his face more uncontrollably. "I've never killed anything before, James. What if it's just a little rabbit or something, I don't wanna hurt it."

"Well, what if it's not!" James yelled.

As a deep-pitched, otherworldly growl came from behind the bush and grew with intensity to an almost thunderous level, they no longer needed to wonder. The growl quickly ebbed, leaving only its echo to ripple through the forest. From the airless quiet that followed, the phantom spoke. "I can see you now, and I will taste you soon." The thing spoke in a demonic voice so chilling it could scare the spots off a leopard. "I'm coming for you, and there's no one here to help you," it heartlessly added.

Before the creature could say one more creepy word, Kalan liberated the stone from the pouch's keep and sent it screaming toward the shadows. "THWOP!" The load most assuredly hit its mark.

"I got it, James…I got it!"

The next sound the boys heard could not be described with words. Suffice it to say that the worst unearthly wail imagined would not come close.

"RUN, JAMES, RUN!" Kalan shouted

Kalan took off with the speed of a cheetah, and James followed close behind. If he were any closer in fact, they'd be attached; but as fast as they ran, they somehow knew it wouldn't be fast enough. The creature would surely catch them.

Kalan and James took turns passing each other on the path, yelling all the way.

"Where is it, Kalan? Where is it...is it close!?"

"Don't look back, James...just run!"

But the creature would not be denied. It swept through the forest like a raging fire, mowing down the bushes as it screamed and caught up with the boys in a heartbeat.

From the corner of his eye, Kalan could see the familiar hellblazer tear past him with ease. Kalan scanned the path before him, but saw no end in sight. He knew there would be no chance of reaching a clearing this time, no possibility of escape.

Time was up for the boys and they watched in horror as the phantom figure leaped from the thicket with an explosive growl and landed onto the path, less than ten yards before them, with an earthshaking "BOOM!"

The boys came to a screeching halt, with Kalan falling to his knees.

"Get up, Kalan, quick!" James cried, finally handing him back his sword.

Kalan quickly grabbed the weapon from his trusted friend as he fumbled to return his slingshot to his back pocket. There would be no time, this time, to search for a perfect stone.

Chapter 22

Monster Revealed

The shadowy presence slowly pushed itself up from all fours to its hind feet with a low threatening growl that vibrated so strongly, Kalan could actually feel it in his chest.

The boys suddenly realized that this was the monstrous image they saw in their daydream. Frozen with terror, the boys could only stare in awe at what had risen before them. At last revealed, they could not believe what they were looking at. Were their eyes deceiving them? Could this really be happening? What stood hunched, snarling and drooling in front of them turning their blood ice cold, was a huge werewolf.

Surely this can't be real, Kalan thought to himself.

These creatures of the night are mere folklore and myth, born out of the dark shadows; they were the stuff of movies and superstition. It was so difficult for the boys to comprehend, yet impossible to deny, what was standing right before their very eyes. They were in shock. The sight and the sound and the smell of this thing sent their young still-developing brains into sensory overload. Oh the smell…a heavy, dirty musk-like stink.

"Kalan, are we dreaming?" James wished, but knew differently.

But before Kalan could utter a word through his quivering lips, the creature let out a deep evil laugh and then immediately stopped and without as much as a grin snorted, "Do I look like a dream to you?"

It was huge, standing nearly eight feet tall. Its arms, which were held close to its body, were bent up at the elbows. Its front paws armed with sharpened three-inch long blood red claws, hung eerily from its muscled wrists. Its massive head, as if too heavy to be properly supported, jutted out from its monstrous cursed body.

"What do you want from us?" Kalan squeaked.

"Do not pretend you know me not, young knights," it snarled as venomous spit flew. "Too long have I waited for this moment," it scowled, showing its teeth. "I shall wait no longer!"

It then began to creep slowly and deliberately towards the boys. How eerie it was, the way the wolf-beast tiptoed, leaning his massive torso precariously forward. The earth trembled with each thunderous step the wolf took as it headed for the boys.

As the devil-wolf came within five yards of them, Kalan raised his sword in defiance and screamed as boldly as he could, hoping it would muster up the courage needed to stand up to this creature, "Don't come any closer, you smelly fur ball!"

The monster stopped dead in its tracks, which then gave James a slight surge of confidence. That was shattered immediately, however, when the wolf let out another demonic, hideous laugh.

"Do you think a child's plastic sword can frighten me?" It laughed again, "Do not insult me, little man—tainted blood of Cathul."

"Cathul?" Kalan couldn't believe his ears. "How do you know about Cathul?"

"I grow weary of this game," the monster snorted, "and you are in need of a miracle, for that worthless toy you hold in your hand, could not pierce a squirrel's skin let alone MY LEATHERY HIDE!" it screamed.

"Well, I guess we'll just have to find out, won't we!" Kalan countered, as disrespectfully as possible, catching the monster completely off guard.

The werewolf just stood there, motionless, in disbelief. How dare this half-pint squat feed the fire?

"Yes," the wolf slowly burned. "I guess we will...NOW!"

In the blink of an eye, the wolfman flew across the safehold between them and was literally face to face with Kalan. As the boy gasped, his lungs filled with the putrid stink of the creature's breath, and before Kalan had time to swing his weapon, the monster grabbed it from the boy and tossed it to the ground.

"You insolent pup! You think you are a match for me?"

James rushed the demon, but caught the back of his mighty paw instead, which sent the boy sailing through the air landing him in a bush several feet away.

"I'll deal with you next, boy. Do you think your blood is any better than his? It is worse! I will make sure that you and your mongrel swine blood stay out of this once and for all!" it screamed at James. Then in a flash, it grabbed Kalan by the throat with one hand and lifted the boy up six feet off the ground.

As Kalan squirmed and gasped for air, the werewolf spoke again, "and now, ignorant child, I'm going to release your spirit to the shadows of the forest and let them deal with you as they wish. Just as I did with "The Great Cathmor..." he said mockingly, "...many centuries ago. Then I will become king, and my father's curse will be fulfilled! You may have defeated me before, little knight, but now...your time is up!"

Just as the hellwolf inhaled deeply and began to raise its huge deadly paw to silence the boy forever, it suddenly stopped. Something was happening. A slight breeze began to blow again, barely stirring the leaves. It picked up quickly, strangely. The beast immediately dropped the boy to the ground, and cocked his massive skull, lifting his right ear to the heavens.

James scurried over to help his friend who was still trying to catch his breath. "Are you okay, Kalan?" he quietly asked, placing his arm around his best buddy.

"What's going on?" Kalan asked, dazed from the lack of oxygen.

"I don't know, but do you hear that...do you hear that sound, Kalan?" They too turned their attention skyward.

"SILENCE!" The beast demanded as it closed its evil eyes to listen more intently.

It was obvious to the boys that whatever it was that was coming, was making the wolfman very skittish and anxious. Could it be possible that this terrifying manslayer, this raging hellhound may actually be afraid of something? Kalan and James sure hoped so.

The wind began to pick up, but this wasn't your ordinary type of wind. This had intention. This had a rhythm of its own...a pulse.

"HHWOOO...HHWOOO...HHWOOO...HHWOOO..."

The leaves from the forest floor began to stir and then suddenly swirl up into little tornadoes, only to die again; while the full thick mane of the beast was swept back from his giant head one second only to lie relaxed, though tousled, the next.

James tried desperately to get Kalan to his feet hoping to escape while the wolf's attention was being diverted, but unfortunately the boy had not yet recovered from the monster's chokehold.

As the sound grew stronger, closer, the beast became more and more agitated, almost tormented. Suddenly, there was a powerful gust and the sound of creaking and cracking as the towering pines began to bend. There was no longer any doubt...the wolfman knew exactly what was happening, and with a bloodcurdling howl towards the heavens above, braced itself for the worst.

Chapter 23

A Sight to Behold

With a blast of wind, the treetops magically parted, allowing what little light there was left from the afternoon sun to shine through.

What happened next sent both boys springing to their feet. What they saw through their squinting eyes staggered their imagination. A gigantic owl diving through the trees with incredible speed, its enormous head perfectly in line with its target…the devilhound!

An ear piercing mournful wail from the beast didn't stop the silent, determined flight of this glorious raptor. Too long had this confrontation been in the making. But to the boys, not soon enough would it be over.

Keeping its eye on the beast up until the very last second, just before contact, the great owl quickly pulled its head back while thrusting its huge bony feet forward. Razor sharp talons spread wide, increasing its chance for a successful strike. "WHAM!"

The talons ripped into the werewolf's chest and locked into place, pushing the beast back at least fifteen feet from the boys. The force of the impact was so strong, it stunned the wolf. The monster groaned, and its wordless pleas escalated into screams of terror and agony, his death song. Feathers and fur flew as the pitiful creature fought back, but to no avail. It was no match for the magnificent rescuer.

The wingspan of this owl was beyond belief, being fully revealed as the enchanted bird lifted the monster some twenty feet off the ground only to release it, plummeting to the forest floor with a thundering, "BOOM!"

The devil lay breathless…dead still.

While the miracle bird hovered high above its kill, the boys watched with astonishment as its massive flapping wings seemed to go right through the trees…as if they were ghostly appendages.

Before the boys could even think of running, the magnificent being floated effortlessly down to the ground and landed right in front of them. They stood there speechless as they watched the extraordinary wings fold softly against the giant's beautifully feathered body with a velvety whoosh.

The boys seemed to be drawn into a world deep within the owl's eyes—so calming and loving. Such a change from the terror they felt just seconds before. At that moment, they knew that all was well.

"Are we dreaming?" Kalan asked James in a soft airy voice, hypnotized by the vision.

"That depends on what you consider a dream, little friend," the great animal replied in a deep, soothing voice.

"You can talk too?" James asked, a bit startled. "That's so awesome!"

"What...I mean who are you?" asked Kalan, snapping out of the spell.

"My name is Braxus," he answered proudly. "I am the guardian of this forest realm, protector of the innocents."

Chapter 24

A Lesson in Time Travel

The boys stood amazed and delighted as the giant owl explained his magical story to them. Several minutes of wonder passed as his explanation of the miraculous transformation, how he was brought into being, unfolded. He told them of his home before the great fire, and where he lived now. He spoke of a place that lies just in the middle, between the dream world and the waking world, where dreams and fantasy are just as real as reality. A place called Potentia…where anything is possible.

"I live in the shadowy mist that surrounds the two worlds," he said with calm authority.

As the boys listened, spellbound, the gentle giant finally reached the end of his enchanted tale, and posed to them a puzzling question. "Would you like to visit your dream kingdom," he asked, "your world of fantasy and endless possibilities? It is a world where fantasy and reality collide."

Kalan and James looked at each other as if to say, *can you believe what's happening here?*

"What do you mean?" Kalan asked the great owl, trying his best not to get over excited. "You can take us there?"

"Alas, my dear little friends, I cannot."

His words fell heavily upon the boys, quickly deflating their hopes and excitement. To think that they were so close to seeing another world, actually visiting their fantasy world, only to have the rug pulled out from under them.

Feeling a bit dejected, they both sighed, as the owl spoke again, "I cannot take you there, but I can show you the way."

"Alright!" James shouted without hesitation.

"Awesome!" Kalan agreed. "How? When?"

"Follow me," the owl said as he turned and walked just past the lifeless mass of muscle and fur that had threatened the boy's lives just a short time ago.

As the boys passed the creature's corpse, something caught Kalan's eye. It was shiny, round and gold, and he knew immediately what it was. The bad news...it was lying in the palm of the werewolf's leathery paw.

"My watch," Kalan whispered. Keeping his eyes focused on the prize, he slowly and carefully leaned over to grab it, stretching his little arm out as far as it would go.

"Be careful, Kalan," James pleaded, startling his friend.

Kalan's heart skipped a beat. "Shhhh, will ya!" Kalan scolded.

The kids were beyond creeped out, both imagining this evil trickster playing dead, then suddenly coming to life, and reaching up and grabbing the boy.

Kalan took one last slow, deep breath and with the heart and speed of a lion...snatched the watch from the killers clutches, then quickly ran to catch up with Braxus. They both let out a huge sigh of relief once they realized they were free and clear of the monster's grasp.

Thrilled to have the watch his grandpa gave him back in his possession, he kissed it, then opened it to make sure it wasn't broken. "We've been gone exactly forty-five minutes, James," Kalan informed his friend. "We're gonna need to get back soon."

"Seems like we've been gone a week," James replied.

The boys looked up to see the owl standing in front of a very strange looking, twisted and gnarled tree. It's funny how they didn't even notice this incredible tree before...a sight that is surely hard to miss, almost as if it had just appeared out of nowhere. James studied the distorted and crooked specimen. He had never seen anything like it before.

"That is one spooky looking tree, he said. "It looks like it's in pain."

"Yeah, it really does," Kalan agreed, "and I know what kind of tree that is, James," he continued. "Last year my dad took me to a place not far from here called Methuselah Grove in the White Mountains. They had a bunch of these trees there. It's called a Bristlecone Pine, and they're the oldest in the world. The ranger there called them 'the ancient ones' and said that some of them were over four thousand years old."

"You are right my little friend," the owl said as he turned towards the boys. "They are the oldest living things on the planet. Some may be thousands of years older than the oldest Giant Sequoia. Many of the Bristlecones living today were around when the great pyramids of Egypt were being built and were thousands of years old when the man Jesus was born."

"Now," Braxus continued, "I would like you both to meet a very special friend of mine," he said as he slowly turned back toward the tree and bowed with great respect. "His name is Titan. He is well over six thousand years old, and he comes and goes as he pleases."

"Comes and goes as he pleases?" Kalan repeated.

The boys turned toward each other with puzzled looks, as if to say, *what the heck is that supposed to mean?* But as soon as Kalan turned back to ask the question, the great owl moved to the side and away from the tree revealing something that commanded the boys' immediate and complete attention. There, in front of them, on Titan's enormous ancient trunk, was a strange looking knot in the shape of what appeared to be an old skeleton keyhole.

"Read aloud what is written before you, and heed its direction," said the great owl.

Clueless, the boys just stared at the knot in the tree, then at each other, then back at Titan. They both turned to the mighty owl, confused and a little embarrassed. "What are we supposed to read?" Kalan wanted to know. "There's nothing there," he added respectfully.

"Look again, young knight, but this time…with more than just your eyes," the owl answered. "See with your heart as well, for your eyes alone can deceive you. Fear and self-doubt blind you from true sight and your true nature. See through new eyes, eyes of love. True love will let you see clearly."

Kalan just looked at James again as if to say, *do you have any idea what he's talking about?*

"How do we do that?" James asked.

"Use your memory, young friends…to time travel," the teacher replied.

Still confused, the boys just looked at each other again, then to the owl.

"I'm sorry, but we don't understand," Kalan said.

The great bird took a step closer to the boys and with a soothing, hypnotic voice spoke, "remember a time…a time when your grandmother hugged you and held you so close to her breast, you could hear and feel the beat of her heart. Or a time when you were hurting and she stroked your hair and dried your tears. Think back to a time when your father held you in his arms, and lifted you up towards the heavens, and declared his love for you to the universe. Or when he tucked you into bed. Remember how safe you felt…so secure, as if nothing in the world could ever harm you. Reflect upon those memories, and you will be there," he so patiently responded.

His words sent the boys flying on a motionless, heartfelt journey. All the wonderful loving moments of their childhood…every single one of them, up to the present moment filled their very beings. Without taking a step, they journeyed through time, always aware of the owl's presence and voice as it gently guided them deeper into a place where time…no longer existed.

"Time is an illusion, it is not real. Understand young knights, that in less time than you could possibly measure, you have relived fully what had taken you years to experience in the waking world. All the exact same emotions and feelings, smells and tastes, as when you experienced them for the very first time. Waking time and dreamtime are indeed the same, no difference whatsoever. They are in your mind, your personal perception. What you need to understand is that you are the creators of both. Every time you remember an event, you actually take your body 'time-traveling'."

Tears filled their eyes and streamed down their faces, and through those tears they now saw what the owl taught them to see.

"Look, Kalan!" James yelled with delight.

"I see it, James, I see it!"

Chapter 25

The Scroll of Somnus

There, hanging on Titan—right in front of them, where moments before was just a knothole—they saw an old, yellow parchment scroll. The boys read aloud.

"Silent wings of retribution
hover high but never fail
to swoop down with resolution,
and protect the forest frail

From a township named Valencia,
chosen warriors small yet brave
claim their kingdoms in Potentia.
Evil flees, and time…their slave.

Thrust your sword into the hollow.
Plunge your steel with all your might.
Knight times two will then gain entry.
Worlds merge at the speed of light."

At the bottom of the poem, a single name was written…*Somnus.*

The boys looked at each other for a few moments as they tried to understand its meaning.

"It says thrust your sword into the hollow," Kalan thought out loud. "Thrust your sword into the hollow…into the hollow…hollow…the hole, James!" Kalan excitedly realized.

Without hesitation, they pulled their swords and together thrust them into the peculiar knothole below the scroll with all their might. Instantly two of Titans huge branches swung out like arms and grabbed the boys, pulled them into his trunk and swept them into another world…the world of their dreams.

Chapter 26

A Place Called Potentia

As soon as they appeared in the new land, the tips of their swords fell heavily to the ground from the weight of the cold hard Damascus steel.

"Wow! Real swords!" James shouted, thrilled with the feel of his new blade.

"YYYEEESS!" Kalan exclaimed, just as excited.

Standing beside the same incredible tree but in a completely different, though strangely familiar landscape, the boys looked out at the valley and hillsides beyond.

"James look!" Kalan shouted. "It's Dragonfly's Meadow! Holy cow, James, look…it really is Dragonfly's Meadow, and there's my castle!"

James looked to the ridge just beyond the first hill and saw a beautiful medieval castle, just as Kalan used to describe it when they played. There was a huge ten-foot thick stone wall surrounding the entire fortress, with large round towers placed uniformly and strategically within the structure of the wall. There were arrow slits in the towers, and in the stone wall as well, through which an archer could shoot his arrows at the enemy, without putting himself in great harm. There was a gatehouse at the front of the castle with a huge heavy iron grate that could be quickly lowered to block an intruder's entrance, and beyond that, were two massive wooden doors that could be barred shut from inside. There were gaps in the ceiling above the entrance passage, called murder holes, through which boiling liquids or deadly missiles could be thrown down upon the attackers. Dotting the valley outside and below the castle was a quaint little village made up of several charming thatched-roof cottages, with lots of people milling around attending to their daily business. With hope, James looked over to his right, and in the oak tree filled glen below, he was not disappointed as he spotted his rugged fortress nestled among the trees.

"There's Wolfshire, Kalan!" James could hardly believe his eyes. Nevertheless, there it was, the beautiful stone and wood manor house, exactly how he had imagined it; complete with moat and drawbridge. "...and look down there, Kalan," he added. "It's the Black River Bridge! Oh man, is this awesome or what?"

At that moment, something drew Kalan's attention back to the little town below his castle at Dragonfly's Meadow.

"What on earth is going on doing down there?" Kalan asked keeping his eyes glued on the strange activity below. "Look at them all, James. They're going crazy down there."

The villagers looked panicked and confused. All of them were running around, bumping into each other as if under attack, and the boys could hear their distant screams. It was mass chaos down there, but there was very good reason for their madness. All but a few villagers ran inside their homes, and one in particular caught

Kalan's eye. He seemed to be shouting something at the boys, while pointing to the sky just above and beyond the bridge.

"Flag-on? What the heck is that supposed to mean? It sounds like he's shouting Flagon or Fragin. I can't make out what he's saying, James, can you?"

James listened carefully but with no luck. He just shook his head with frustration.

"Look up there, James. What does that look like to you?" Kalan pointed to the spot in the sky, where the villager had just indicated, which was growing larger with each passing second. "Wait a minute. Is that...that couldn't possibly be what I think it is...could it?"

"I guess that depends on what you think it...holy cow!" James shouted.

Both coming to the same realization at precisely the same time, they turned, faced each other and yelled, "DRAGON!"

How strange and exciting it was to see this odd, scaled beauty commanding attention as it soared through the blue, cloud dappled, sky. This ancient mythical creature, covered with bright shiny emerald green and bronze scales was, by the way, heading right for them!

"Get your sword ready, Kalan!" James shouted, lifting his solid steel blade chest high and back with no problem at all.

"I wish I had my shield!" Kalan yelled, raising his massive claymore—one of the largest swords in the world—with equal ease. At that moment, the boys heard something fall to the ground beside

Kalan's feet. Kalan glanced down to find the most exquisite shield, beyond anything he could ever imagine. It was bright gold in color and highly polished. Engraved on the face was the young knight's family crest, two rather imposing Scottish highlander claymores majestically crossing each other with a perfectly scripted "O" embossed on top of them, which was skillfully hand-tooled into the middle. A flawless English braid, which was hammer and chiseled along the entire outer edge, finished off the front of the shield. All that graced the back of the armor were two, three-inch wide leather straps for handles, which Kalan immediately put to use.

"This is unbelievable," Kalan muttered to himself, as he held the shield and sword in ready mode. "I just can't believe this is happening. I just...this is unbelievable!"

The dragon was fast, already just a few hundred yards out. The force of the powerful wings sweeping down, then forward, back, then up...scooping the air and thrusting the beast upwards and forwards, was remarkable. Such a massive amount of energy was needed just to keep it aloft. An impressive sight to behold to say the least.

It takes better than a few years of practice to build the extremely powerful flight muscles needed to lift a heavy draconian body off the ground, so this one must have been around for a while, because it seemed particularly gifted at it.

As the monster closed in on the boys, Kalan tilted his new shield toward the sun, and reflected its blinding light directly into the dragon's bright green eyes. Caught off guard, the dragon quickly turned its head away from the glare, causing it to briefly lose lift. Taking only a moment to regain its original flight path, the dragon let out a hellish roar, belched out yellow and white-hot flames, and continued to advance on the boys.

"Hide beneath my shield, James, quick!" Kalan yelled.

The boys huddled close to the ground as Kalan covered them with the armor plate. Kalan sneaked a quick peek around the shield's edge, only to see the monster lizard diving straight towards the boys, with flames shooting from its mouth and nostrils.

"Hang on, James," Kalan screamed, "I have a feeling this isn't gonna be pretty!"

The boys could tell the creature was upon them as the grass around them burned, and the shield became hot. As the heat became almost unbearable, James instinctively thrust his steel into the burning air above the shield, and slashed into the dragon's delicate wing membrane.

"I got it, Kalan...I cut it with my sword!" James said, as he burst out from under the armor.

Kalan joined his friend, as they watched the dragon spiral slowly downward into the valley just beyond Wolfshire.

"Did you kill it?"

"I don't know," James replied. "It felt kind of weird, like I didn't really hit much."

"His wing has been torn, and his pride...bruised," a voice said from behind the boys.

They turned quickly to see the huge owl standing behind them.

"Braxus! How long have you been there?" Kalan asked, thrilled to see his new teacher and friend.

"Only a moment, Kalan," he answered.

They all watched as the mighty flying lizard hit the ground with considerable force.

"It will take a while for that dragon's wing to heal," Braxus informed them, "and when it does, I assure you, he too, will be looking for you both."

"Great, just what we need, more trouble!" Kalan said. "Haven't we been through enough already?!"

"He is not going to be very happy with you," Braxus added. "He has a very long walk home."

The boys turned and looked up at the owl, who seemed to be smiling, and they burst into laughter.

"Way to go James, you brought down a dragon! Can you believe that? Man, that's so awesome!"

"I couldn't have done it without you, buddy," James said with a smile, as he patted Kalan on the shoulder. "We make a great team."

"Best friends, brave knights!" Kalan shouted, as he held his sword high into the air.

"Best friends, brave knights," James echoed, as their weapons united.

"I would like you two brave knights to come with me," Braxus gently interrupted. "I have something very, very important to tell you."

The huge bird stretched out its enormous wings and invited the boys to climb aboard. "Would you like to fly with me?" he asked.

"Are you kidding?" Kalan answered, with the biggest smile James had ever seen on his friend's face. "You Bet!"

Braxus helped the boys climb onto his back, with a slight push from his powerful wings. "Hang on to my feathers, little friends, you're safe with me," he said as he took off and soared down into the valley below and landed just this side of the Black River Bridge. It would have taken Kalan and James at least ten minutes to travel the distance it took Braxus seconds to cover.

The boys looked at each other as if to say, *is that it?* But before they could voice their disappointment to Braxus regarding the brevity of the flight, they were cut off by what they thought was someone calling their names.

They turned to see several townsfolk cheering and applauding them as they came out of their homes in the village and approached the bridge. "Hooray for Lord Kalan! Hooray for Sir James! Hooray! They beat the dragon, hooray!"

"Lord Kalan?" Kalan repeated as if trying to solve a riddle.

"Sir James?" James said just as baffled as his friend.

"What the heck is going on, Braxus?" Kalan asked. "Who are these people, and how do they know our names? And why are they calling me Lord?"

"Yeah, and me, Sir?"

The great bird smiled at the boys before turning his attention to Kalan. His mighty wings unfolded wide.

"Because this is your kingdom, young knight—young king," he said. "The Kingdom of Keeral."

Chapter 27

A Tale of Three Cities

"Listen carefully, my little friends, to what I am about to tell you," the great owl began, as he guided the young knights down from his back. "My words are not meant to frighten you, but I must caution you both. There is an evil in this world that would wish to harm you."

"You mean, like the dragon, Braxus?" Kalan timidly asked.

"The dragon is nothing compared to that of which I speak, young knight. In your world, where fantasy and reality intertwine, there are things I can defeat but cannot destroy. Only you have been given that power."

The boys listened attentively, as the owl spoke again of a miraculous transformation. Only this time, however, he was not speaking of his magical change, but of the evil mutation of the shadow dweller. The creature that hunted them through the forest in the other world, he told them, pursued them in this realm as well.

"His name is Phelan, a skinwalker or shapeshifter, and a powerful sorcerer in his own right. He will do anything and everything in his power to bring your life to an end, Kalan."

"Me? But why me, Braxus, what did I ever do to him?" Kalan asked.

"You are the chosen one, young knight, and he is well aware of that. He has been waiting patiently through the centuries…for you, Kalan—as I have. The curse of his father brought him into being, and has lasted this long. You are the only one, in thousands of years, who can break it. You must kill him, young king; for Phelan seeks revenge, and evil demands he rule not only over Keeral, but all of Potentia."

Kalan just looked at him, fearful and confused. Yet one more thing, within the last few days, the boys didn't understand.

He motioned with his great wing for them to be seated. "Please sit down, both of you, and I will tell you briefly of how all this began. It is a story about the kingdom of Keeral, and your ancestors, Kalan; and yours too, James—and even mine. It is a story of murder and friendship, curses and kings. It is also a story of how our lives intertwine, and of how we three are much closer than either one of you could ever possibly imagine."

Braxus began with what the boys already knew, how the wicked Braedon had murdered his own father to gain control of the kingdom. How Braedon became the twisted, evil soul he was, however, the great bird did not know.

"Your great ancestor, Cathul, killed the sorcerer king and gained control of Keeral."

"But how, Braxus? If Braedon was such a great sorcerer, how could Cathul, an ordinary man, beat him?"

"By finding and piercing the wizard's heart, which you must understand was truly a miraculous feat in itself. For you see, Braedon's black heart...was made of stone. But that my young friend, is a whole other story in itself and will have to wait for another time, I am afraid," Braxus told him.

The great bird then turned towards the villagers who had come to hail the warriors. "Please, return to your village and homes, gentle people," he said with wings spread wide. "What I have to say, is for these young warrior's ears alone." As the people began to disperse, he kindly thanked them, then turned back towards the boys and continued.

"Before Braedon died, however, he cursed Cathul and his family—your family, Kalan; 'I will not die, you fool! My spirit will live on in a boy who will join your ranks, and live for me...through you, as I slumber through the ages!' he screamed with his last gasp of sweet air, just before Cathul beheaded him, assuring the tyrant's final sleep."

"Cathul ruled over a grateful, peaceful kingdom for many years to come before falling in love and marrying a beautiful, young village girl named Tawnisha, who became with child soon thereafter. There were difficulties during the months to come, however, as one day while the king's physician was attending to the new queen, he placed his hearing devise to her swollen belly and announced, 'I hear the hearts of two beating, my queen.' Three months later, Tawnisha gave birth to their first-born son, Cathmor. They were amazed how quickly and easily he entered the world, without a sound; no pain or bother whatsoever for the loving new mother, a perfectly blessed birth indeed, they all agreed. The second child, on the other hand, was nothing of the sort. No, far from it I am sorry to say. His delivery was pure torturous hell. Seven long days the queen labored, howling with pain. She could not eat or drink, nor could she sleep; seven endless days and nights, twisted with the screams of agony that echoed through the kingdom and lingered there like a dark heavy fog that refused to leave. The thought of Braedon's curse drifted in and out of Cathul's mind like a taunting spirit, and on that seventh night, the queen's suffering at last came to an end, when Phelan, their second son was born—breach; that is, feet first. Shortly thereafter, the sweet, beautiful Tawnisha died."

A single tear dropped from Kalan's eye, which did not go unnoticed by the great owl.

Braxus continued, "a lesser man would have truly hated the child for taking the life of his soul mate, his wife, his one and only true love—but not Cathul. He was far too good a man, his heart, pure." Braxus looked at Kalan with such deep, heartfelt emotion and said, "You do indeed share the heart, soul and blood of the great Cathul, my young friend; of that, there is no doubt. Compassion—" he sighed, lightly touching the boy's shoulder with the tip of his wing, "a knightly strength that has truly been underestimated through the ages."

Kalan felt honored and proud that the owl compared him to such a great man, and he smiled as Braxus continued the tale.

"Cathul tried his very best to raise both of his boys with the same amount of love, respect and attention, for he knew that is what his dear Tawnisha would have wanted. He quickly realized, however, that would not be possible. Phelan would not let that happen. Phelan continually rejected his father's loving attempts and absolutely hated his brother Cathmor. The difference between the children was great, and obvious to all who were exposed to them.

Cathmor, always the thinker, was kind and respectful, and filled with a love of life. Phelan, on the other hand, was the complete opposite—filled with rage, greedy and cruel.

On many occasions his father would be absolutely heartbroken after finding his deviant son hurting, even torturing, some of the village creatures. Cathul despised such cruelty, and tried to convince the boy that his behavior was not only wrong, but against all that he stood for as the king, and as a man, but to no avail. The strange behavior not only continued, it became much worse. When Phelan reached the age of ten, he began to disappear into the forest for days, even weeks at a time, only to be more distant upon his return. One night, midway through his tenth year, after watching him vanish into the darkness of the forest, the king went into the boys sleeping chambers and found the first of many animals Phelan had butchered, lying there, mutilated and lifeless on a strange type of alter, which sat next to a window that faced the forest. The king was horrified with his discovery.

On a number of occasions the king secretly sent one of his best men to keep an eye on the child, to find out more information, but the young boy proved impossible to follow. There was talk throughout the kingdom that someone, or something in the woods was educating the boy in the ways of the black arts; and at the age of thirteen, Phelan left his fathers home, never to return. The king found out some years later that his estranged son was establishing a kingdom of his own, no more than two weeks travel, by horse from Keeral—called Mahl. Cathul knew his son well enough to know, however, that this kingdom would not be one built upon honor and respect of life. Instead, Phelan's kingdom would be raised from the cornerstone of greed and hate and mortared with the blood of the innocents. He also knew that eventually, Phelan would rise up against him and Cathmor and try to either take over the kingdom of Keeral, or destroy it all together."

Kalan and James were completely engrossed in the tale, and couldn't take their eyes off the great owl as he went on with the story.

"Phelan eventually had a son, named Darcus, though no one knows how. He never married; in fact he was rarely ever seen outside his castle walls. It was rumored that on occasion, Phelan would employ the services of a hobgoblin, named Robin Goodfellow to do his dirty work."

"Robin Goodfellow?" Kalan freaked out. "That was the guy who pretended to be the ranger, James—remember?"

"Are you kidding me, how could I forget that weirdo?"

"You should avoid that creature at all costs," Braxus quickly interrupted. "He is evil and he is a thief, and will only bring you harm. Listen carefully," he warned, "if you do ever cross his path again, be careful not to let him get close enough to take something personal from you, for if he does, he could cast an evil spell over you that would be difficult to remove."

James shook his head with disgust. "I'll bet he took your watch, Kalan," he said. "He stole it when he fell against you, remember? That's probably how Phelan got it! I'll bet you anything that's what happened. Man, what a jerk!"

"Yeah," Kalan agreed. "You're probably right, buddy. I knew I didn't just drop it."

Braxus continued his story about Phelan and his association with the wicked sprite. "One dark moonless night he sent the mischievous imp into the village outside his castle. There, Robin stole the boy from one of the village women, while she slept. The woman woke to her baby's cry, just in time to see him being carried off into the shadows by what she called 'a devil spirit.' The next morning the baby's father and some other men from the village searched high and low for the child, but found nothing, except for the tracks of the strange creature. The footprints were seen in all kinds of inaccessible places—on the tops of houses and narrow walls, in gardens and courtyards enclosed by high rock walls and fences, as well as in the open fields that surrounded the village. Stranger still was the way the prints interchanged from human to dog or wolf and then to some sort of cloven-hoofed animal like a goat or deer. Whenever the prints took animal form, however, they were only in twos, as if the animal was walking on its hind legs the whole time; a true master shapeshifter indeed. Phelan raised the child as his own, and in turn, passed his wicked, evil ways on to him.

Now, years passed, and Cathul lived to be an old man without ever seeing his second born again, nor his stolen child. The great king died peacefully in the arms of his devoted, first-born son, but not before he was able to know and love his beautiful grandson, Torin; Cathmor's only child."

"Torin? Wait a minute. That's the name engraved on the sword that my dad has. Is that the same Torin, Braxus?" Kalan asked.

"It is indeed, Kalan. The sword your father now possesses was a gift of thanks from Delyn, leader of a third village called Tayma. It just so happens that on a beautiful day, not unlike today—with a single arrow, Torin, son of Cathmor, saved the life of Delyn's firstborn son from the murderous hands of Darcus. Delyn and his son presented the sword to Cathmor and Torin during a fire ceremony in which they vowed to protect the O'Shel clan for as long as they lived."

"So Torin was a hero because he saved the life of Delyn's son, right?" Kalan asked, thinking back on the fireside talk he had with his dad and James.

"Oh yes," the owl answered, gazing off toward the horizon, as if fondly remembering a moment from long, long ago. "Torin was a great hero, without question."

"Wow, that's so cool," Kalan said, beaming with pride for the ancestor he never knew. Then after thinking for a moment he added, "hey, you forgot to tell us Delyn's son's name. What was his name?" Kalan asked, looking up at the huge raptor, waiting anxiously for a response.

"Braxus," the great owl replied. "Delyn was my father."

Chapter 28

The Fury of The Berserker

They went without shields, and were mad as dogs or wolves...and were as strong as bears or bulls...and neither fire nor steel would deal with them; and this is what is called the fury of the berserker.

—The Ynglinga Saga—1225 AD

"It was you that Torin saved," Kalan realized, staring up in awe at the miraculous man-bird.

"Yes it was, little king. I was in my fourteenth year at the time. Many, many years ago..."

In fact almost two thousand years had passed since the day Torin saved Braxus' life, just outside the village of Tayma, where Braxus was born and raised—not far from the kingdom of Keeral.

Through The Great Forest, which bordered Keeral on the west, just past a vast clearing known as Meadow Golden, was an enormous oak forest called Odinwood. Deep within the heart of that forest, the village of Tayma could be found. The people who dwelled in the village were known as the Keltoi by other civilizations of that era. The first recorded encounter with the Keltoi, which means barbarian, dates back to around four hundred years before the birth of Christ, but the Keltoi were around for many centuries before that. They have been greatly misunderstood and misrepresented through the ages, and even now, their reputation as being murderous savages could not be further from the truth. They were in fact a deeply religious, very loving and extremely protective people. That being said, however, there was good reason for fearing them and believing the rumors that spread throughout the lands regarding their magical shape changing abilities, for that was absolutely founded in truth.

Before a battle the warriors of the tribe, known as berserkers, would engage in a ritual, in which they would whip themselves into an incredible frenzy after drinking the blood of a freshly killed bear. It was believed that they not only gained the fierceness of the animal, but all of its incredible strength as well. Flooded by a mysterious force, it was during the peak of this wild intense fit of fury, which could last for several hours, that their bodies would actually change, or morph, preparing them for war. It was truly a miraculous transformation, believed to be a gift from their god, Odin. As the morphing began, their ears would become smaller and pull closer to their heads, while their hair would shorten to the point of making it impossible to grab during hand-to-hand combat. Their feet would widen for incredible stability, and their skin would thicken making it virtually impossible for an enemy sword to pierce. Last, but certainly not least, their testicles would actually withdraw up into their pelvic cavity, assuring the future of the warrior tribe.

The berserker scream could be heard from miles away as they ran naked into the heat of battle with nothing more than their sword. While in their frenzied state, they were so strong and oblivious to pain that nothing and no one was too much for them to handle.

As soon as they were out of it, however, and the fury had left them, they became much weaker than normal and extremely vulnerable for attack. Unfortunately, the weakened state could last for hours, even days depending upon how old the warrior was and how long they had been in the frenzy.

A youth did not just become a berserker warrior by blood alone. Even though the boy's blood carried the magical abilities, first there needed to be an initiation, a right of passage that he had to endure in order to be accepted into the warrior clan. The boy would be sent into the forest, alone. There, for the first time, he would need to work himself into the frenzy of the berserker, without the influence of the other warriors. While in the berserker state, he would have to battle and kill a bear, then bring the skin home, before earning his place among the warriors.

This initiation was the reason Braxus was alone when Phelan's son, Darcus, and five of his men attacked him. He had already located the den of a bear and was well into working himself into the berserker frenzy he needed to accomplish his task when an axe, thrown by one of Darcus' men, came whizzing by his ear and slammed into the tree in front of him. Before Braxus had the time to turn completely around, one of the thugs was already upon him, and the bloody battle had begun. Now needless to say, a fourteen-year-old boy against five adult, seasoned warriors is not very good odds; and if Braxus had not already worked himself into the berserker fury, he surely would have been easily defeated. However, he was in the frenzy, which made the odds not only different, but in his favor. Because even a child berserker in warrior mode, is stronger and more ferocious than three men combined.

Darcus and his men could not believe the fierceness, strength and speed of the child. In one swift motion Braxus blocked the sword of his opponent, grabbed his shirt, slashed his throat and threw him to the ground, all the while letting out a scream so frightening, it literally paralyzed two of the other warriors. That was indeed unfortunate for them, because while they were struck motionless with terror, the young berserker plunged his short sword into the heart of one, and then turned around and sliced through the gut of the other. It was much too late then for those three evil henchmen to realize what a stupid mistake they had made. Not too late for a fourth though, who went running back into the forest like a scared little rabbit.

Braxus turned to face the fifth and largest of the group, a giant of a man, who was by far the biggest creature Braxus had ever seen in his entire life. His hair and beard were long and filthy, knotted with the blood and mud from years of battle. He must have been at least seven feet tall and weighed over four hundred pounds, all of which was wielding a hammer-type weapon large enough to bring down a Brahma bull.

With a whoosh, the huge hammer swung around and struck the young boy in the side, knocking him to the ground with ease. The force of the blow was incredible and would have killed an ordinary man let alone a child, but Braxus was not ordinary, nor was he finished. He spun around and while still on the ground, sliced through the tendon on the back of the giant's leg, just behind the knee. Not unlike watching a huge Red Wood being cut down, the giant went crashing to the ground. Before he could push his enormous body up to his knees, an exhausted Braxus rolled toward him and thrust his blade into the man's side. The sword sliced between the giant's ribs, piercing his heart.

Darcus, like his father, was cunning, as are most evil creatures. He just stood there watching, while the others struggled and died, and waited for the perfect opportunity to end the fight on his own terms. As Braxus was finishing off the giant, Darcus quietly positioned himself behind the boy, sword held high, ready to cut off the head of the young berserker.

"Die you freak!" Darcus screamed, but before he could bring the sword down upon the neck of the unsuspecting Braxus, he froze for a heartbeat, and then fell to the ground...dead.

Braxus crawled over to the limp, twitching body of Darcus and there, sticking out of the back of the evil prince, but buried deep, was an arrow—still trembling from the impact. Braxus, magic frenzy fading and totally exhausted from the battle, pushed himself up to his knees with all his might, and then slowly to his feet. He turned in the direction from which the arrow came, and in the distance, at the edge of Meadow Golden where The Great Forest began, stood a boy who couldn't have been more than ten years old, standing next to a beautiful jet-black horse and holding a bow above his head. It was Torin, heir to the throne of Keeral.

Braxus could hardly believe his eyes. A boy, with perfect timing, had undeniably saved his life, and not a berserker child either. Not that Braxus minded what village the boy who saved his life was from; he could've been from Mars for all Braxus cared. It was just very unusual back then for anyone outside your own village to lift a finger to help. Thank Odin for Torin! He could have easily just watched the struggle from the safety of the forest without lifting a finger, but he chose not to. A powerful word, choice. Torin, a ten-year-old boy, did what most others would not have done in his position; watched and kept to themselves, not gotten involved, maybe even run away. Not Torin, he chose to act and do what he thought was right, no matter what the consequences may have been, the sign of a true hero and leader. This was indeed a new era—two cities not far in distance or boundary, but so different in belief, religion and way of life, brought together by chance, and the spirit of two young boys.

With a tear in his eye and his heart filled with gratitude and relief, an overwhelmed Braxus lifted his bloody short sword high into the air and waved to the boy in thanks for the incredible gift he had just been given.

Kalan and James sat in silent awe, staring up at the great owl, completely mesmerized by his tale. Kalan was so proud to hear of his great ancestor's bravery and skill. To think that he shared the same blood as this boy-hero, brought a sense of importance to his life that he had never felt before.

Braxus continued, "needless to say, once Phelan heard of his son's death, he vowed revenge. Phelan, being the wicked one he was, took it one step further, however. He would not only retaliate upon Torin, but he would make sure every man woman and child from both the Kingdom of Keeral and Tayma were murdered and both cities were destroyed. Phelan, the sorcerer king, is the one who conjured up the terrible fire that has been referred to as 'The Great Cleansing Blaze,' which destroyed the land and almost everything and everyone in it. Knowing that Phelan would seek his revenge, and knowing it would be something horrible, I gave Torin, with Cathmor's permission, to my brother Ulf who took him far away to safety."

"Over the next several days, Cathmor and my father, Delyn, knowing that Phelan would attack, discussed a strategy to combine forces and do away with the heartless tyrant forever. No one ever really fully understood the extent of Phelan's evilness or the scope of his power, and certainly never imagined that he was strong enough to use his evil to lay waste to the land and exterminate the people. However, Phelan was a self-centered fool and quickly realized that he was nowhere near as powerful as the evil he had released and even he, with all his power, could not escape the fire's wicked fury.

Unfortunately, however, Phelan was spared, but not before he felt the wrath of his own wicked deed. Moments before he burned to death, writhing in horrible pain, Phelan made a pact with the dark forces of the forest, which saved his miserable life, and turned him into the thing he is today. As I was born from the miracle to protect you, your family and all the innocent creatures of the forest through the ages, I was also given the gift of permeation by the Great Mother, that is, being able to pass through the different worlds with ease. So too was the evil one given a twisted, polluted version of the gift from his father and the Shadow Spirit. While in your waking world he assumes the form of the beast you encountered on the trail, here in Potentia he takes human form. He is Phelan, the black knight; and I assure you, you will meet him again. When that time is upon you, you must stay strong and never let fear guide your way."

Braxus knew by the look in Kalan's eyes that he was overwhelmed and frightened. He leaned into the child and placed his enormous wing softly upon his back.

"The spirit of the great warrior king, Cathul is within you, Kalan. His strength, bravery, honor and compassion for his fellow man have been alive in your bloodline for centuries, and it has all been passed down to you. It is up to you, young king to defeat Phelan once and for all, and take your rightful place as King of Keeral, here in Potentia. For if you do not, he will kill you without hesitation, and then evil will surely reign supreme."

"I'm so confused, Braxus," Kalan said.

"Yeah, me too," James nodded.

"I'm sure you are, young knights," the owl replied. "You have been through much this day. But do not worry, as your time passes and we meet again, I will help you to understand."

"Braxus, you said that you were going to tell me something about my family. What does my family have to do with any of this?" James asked.

"More than you could ever possibly imagine my young friend," Braxus replied with a smile. He looked deep into the child's eyes before he continued. "You were born from the blood of the berserker."

"What?" James cried, puzzled and shocked.

Kalan looked over at his best friend with equal amazement.

"That's right," Braxus added. "You and I share the same blood, for you, my dear James, are the descendant of my brother, Ulf. When he took Torin to safety, my father's bloodline also continued. You and I are family, James…separated only by time."

The boys were speechless. It was a day of just too much information being topped off with the knowledge that James was related to a huge magical bird. What do you say to that!

As the boys stared out into the glorious realm beyond their dreams, so beautiful, so perfect and exciting, they shared a few moments of silence. Convinced they had only scratched the surface of their strange new world, but too tired and overwhelmed by the day's events to continue, Kalan asked the great owl, "how do we get home, Braxus, and can we come back here again?"

"You are just as home here, Kalan, as you are on the other side; and you can come and go as you please, from anywhere. This you will both learn in time, and I will help," he answered, "but for now...you can get back the same way you came," the owl said, as he spread his enormous wings, enfolding the boys, "and you can return, the same way, anytime you like."

He gently turned the boys around and led them back to Titan, the enchanted bristlecone pine. But before the young knights performed the same strange ritual that had brought them there, they turned and hugged the great owl...their new friend.

"Thank you, Braxus," they said.

"I will always be here for you," the owl assured them, as he turned to fly away, "for all of the innocent creatures," he added as he lifted himself off the ground. "For as long as I am needed, you can find me here," he said as the wind carried his words back to the boys. "Goodbye, little friends, young knights. Be careful."

The boys watched as Braxus, the owl, soared thousands of feet into the air, beyond the valleys, beyond the hills. Then slowly, without a single flap of his wings, he hovered there for a moment, motionless, before turning his massive body towards the boys. Then, with a burst of white light, which shot out from the middle of his chest and filled the sky, he was instantly transformed into the most beautiful, pure white billowy cloud they, or anyone else, had ever seen.

Chapter 29

Going Home

After several minutes of just staring at the enchanted cloud, the wearied boys looked at each other and smiled. They lifted their swords high into the air, then once again plunged them deep into the magical hole in the tree. In the blink of an eye, they were transported back onto the camp trail where earlier they had left their furry, formidable rival.

"Look, Kalan." James pointed to an opening in the treetops where the sky was peeking through. Just beyond, they saw the brilliant, white cloud hanging motionless in the sky as the other clouds drifted idly by.

"Man, what a day!" an exhausted Kalan sighed.

"Yeah," James agreed. "Boy...I'm really tired."

"I hope my dad's not too worried. He's probably out looking for us," Kalan said, as he pulled his watch from his pocket to see just how much trouble they were in.

"Yeah, he's probably gonna be pretty mad, huh?" James said, as he watched Kalan's eyes light up.

"James look!" Kalan exclaimed, showing his best friend the watch. "Can you believe it? We've still been gone only forty-five minutes! Time stood still, James!"

"Wow. I'll bet we could spend days over there, Kalan, and when we got back, nothing here would be changed. Boy, oh boy, wait till your dad hears about this!"

"What?!" Kalan shouted, "Are you nuts? We can't tell my dad about this. He'd never believe us anyway...nobody would."

"Yeah," James thought, "you're probably right."

"Come on, buddy, let's just get back to the campsite. I'm tired, and I'm starving."

"Yeah, me too. Hey, maybe we can make s'mores around the campfire tonight," James added with a smile, as they turned to make their way back to the camp.

"Whatever you say, berserker boy," Kalan said with a chuckle, playfully elbowing his buddy.

Suddenly, Kalan stopped dead in his tracks. "I just thought of something," he said to his companion in a dead serious tone, "and a major chill just shot down my spine!"

"Oh no...please, Kalan, don't do this to me. Let's just keep going, okay? Come on." James started walking.

"Wait a minute, James...just wait a minute," Kalan said, as if something had just dawned on him.

He looked at James, then turned slowly to look back towards where the wolf's lifeless body was lying. "He's gone, James! Phelan's gone!"

Indeed he was. All that remained was a bit of bloody matted fur, an indentation in the ground where Braxus had dropped the beast, and huge tracks that disappeared into the woods.

"Let's get the heck outta here, James. Let's go!"

The boys ran as fast as they could back to the camp. They both knew they would see this creature again…the evil knight…Phelan. They didn't know where or when, but they were sure of it, just as Braxus said.

None of that seemed to matter now, however. All they could think about was getting back to camp. As the sun began to set, they burst out from the forest into the campsite to the smell of hamburgers grilling over an open fire, and the sound of Kalan's dad whistling as he cooked. They stopped and fell to the ground from exhaustion.

"Hey, good timing!" Kalan's dad shouted, as he fanned the smoke away from his face. "Boy, oh boy, you guys need to hit the trails more often," he teased, "get some exercise. You shouldn't be panting that hard just from a little hike. So, did you guys have fun fighting off evil…whatever?" he asked totally unaware.

The boys just looked at each other, and laughed.

"Yeah, Dad…we sure did," Kalan replied, thrilled to be back.

"Well, pony up to the chuck wagon li'l pardners and feast on the best darn burgers this side 'a the Mississippi," his dad playfully called out in a funny cowboy voice, as he flipped a grilled-to-perfection masterpiece onto a paper plate.

The next hour or so passed easily...eating, laughing and sharing stories 'round the fire. The man-in-the-moon looked down upon the clan, and smiled sweetly as he quietly ascended, brightly adorning the star studded evening sky above.

"It just doesn't get any better than this. What a perfect end to an absolutely perfect day, huh boys?" Kalan's dad sighed, as he poked the fire with a stick he used earlier for roasting marshmallows.

As the boys lay peacefully on their backs, tummies full of burgers and s'mores, with their heads resting comfortably upon their clasped hands, they stared up at the pure white luminous cloud that hovered watchfully, like a doting parent, high above the amber glow of the campsite.

"Well, I guess we'll have to do this more often, huh?" Kalan's dad asked as he began to drift off by the fire.

The boys just looked at each other and shared another smile. All that they had gone through on this day had brought them even closer together as friends. And for now, their secret was safe.

"Sure," James replied with a chuckle.

"Sounds great, Dad," Kalan added with a secure contented sigh, "sounds great."

THE END

978-0-595-37360-4
0-595-37360-7

Printed in the United States
57191LVS00006B/109-129